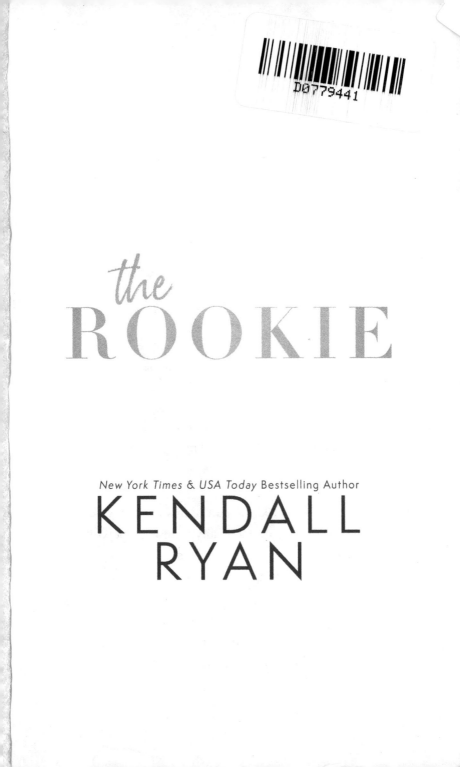

the ROOKIE

New York Times & *USA Today* Bestselling Author

KENDALL RYAN

About the Book

He has everything a man could want. A lucrative hockey contract. Adoring fans. A family who loves him.

But he's about to throw it all away. Logan Tate's name is dominating the headlines for all the wrong reasons. Instead of goals and assists, the talented young defenseman has been racking up fights and suspensions.

I work with athletes who are struggling, but Logan's different. He's not just going to blow his season, but his entire career. And now he can't return to the ice until he deals with his issues, but the stubborn man won't let anyone get close enough to help.

Which is why I packed up and followed him to his family's property in the remote mountains of Colorado. He can't avoid me here.

The only problem?

I can't avoid him either. He's chopping wood and building fires, rescuing my car from snowy ditches, and inviting me to Sunday dinners with his loud extended family. He's a whole lot of man, but beneath all those hard edges is an unexpected tenderness.

Tempted or not, I have to stay out of his bed and get him back to the ice . . . no matter how difficult that might be.

Playlist

"Shy Away" by Twenty One Pilots

"All Time Low" by Monsters, featuring blackbear

"Slow Down" by Gilligan Moss

"Come a Little Closer" by Cage the Elephant

"Teardrop" by Massive Attack

"Fragments" by Thievery Corporation

"Heart on Fire" by Scars on 45

"Love Don't Die" by The Fray

1

LOGAN

The Boston Titans are playing in our home arena, and we're losing. Badly. And I'm a big part of the reason why.

I've managed to screw up on every shift I've taken on the ice—an impressive feat, for sure. Although the first time wasn't my fault. At least, not completely. My stick broke on a pass. Hell, maybe I was being too aggressive, but either way, instead of flying over to our right wing, the puck only wobbled a few feet away and was snatched up by the Avalanche's defense.

That was when they scored their first goal . . . only forty seconds into the game . . . and when everything started to go downhill.

What I know for certain is that my team is losing patience with me. Even our captain, Reeves, who's always supported me, was *this close* to dropping his gloves and pounding me into the ice. I could practically taste his frustration when he growled in my face.

"Come on, Tate. Get your shit together," he hissed as he skated past me.

Of course, this had to happen against our biggest rivals, the Denver Avalanche. And it's my fault we're down by three goals.

"Shit game you're having, yeah?" Bronson, the Avalanche's cocky center, gives me a grin that shows off his missing front tooth.

"Shit *game*? Try shit season." His teammate Raduloff smirks at me, his eyes sparkling with delight.

I grind my teeth against my mouthguard to keep from saying anything. His words sting like only the truth can.

There are no hockey fans holding up signs for me in the stands. No jerseys with my name printed on the back. Not yet, anyway. I'm unproven talent, the new guy on the team. And I'm blowing it every single time I take the ice.

It would help if I could get out of my own head for four fucking seconds. Yet lately, a bunch of confusing thoughts seem to fill my brain—like who I want to be in the NHL, and what I want to be known for. And since I don't have any answers, it's messed with my ability to perform.

At first, I was happy just to be getting ice time, but it quickly became clear that's not enough. I'm up against some of the most talented players in the world, and they're literally skating circles around me. They're the type of guys who are the best in the league and *still* aren't satisfied, and I'm learning that's the mentality you have to have to succeed. It's not enough just to make it. It's not enough that I can skate fast and handle a stick at the same time.

Maybe I don't belong here at all. Maybe I've only been fooling everyone before. Imposter syndrome is alive and well.

Self-doubts like these are always followed by the same somber thought . . . I wish my dad were still around to talk to. Maybe he'd have some insight or words of wisdom. Or maybe he'd just tell me he's proud of me and that everything else will start to fall into place. But all I have now is my memories of him.

At the next face-off circle, Bronson skates past, giving me a little shove. "Don't worry about Tate. He won't be here next year."

"At this rate, he won't be here next *week*," Raduloff says, his tone serious now, less teasing.

Bronson is bounced from the face-off circle and replaced with an angry-looking guy from Russia. What happens next is a blur.

They win the puck, and I move into my zone. Raduloff pokes his stick at my skate, almost tripping me before skating away with a smirk.

I race after him across the ice, white noise screaming in my ears, and tackle him from behind. A stealthy, highly illegal attack he wasn't prepared for.

Raduloff goes down like a sack of potatoes—hard, quick, and without any of the grace he normally has on the ice. When he twists around to fight me off, I get in two solid hits before we're pulled apart and I'm escorted off the ice.

I feel nothing but rage.

• • •

"What the hell were you thinking?" Coach Wilder bellows, jabbing his finger into my chest before taking a step back so he can continue pacing the conference room with frustrated steps.

We're joined by Coach Tanner, and a woman I don't recognize from the league. I'm told she's the head of player safety, so I know this meeting is serious. Which is why I dressed in a suit and arrived twenty minutes early, just to be safe.

That little stunt I pulled on the ice last night cost us the game. I was ejected, and my team had to play five minutes short-handed for the major penalty. The sports reporters had a lot to say about my behavior, me as a player, as a teammate, as a person . . . and none of it was positive.

Wilder pauses and places one hand on the table, leaning toward me. "Raw talent isn't enough to justify *misconduct*. You know that."

"Yes, sir."

"This can't go unpunished."

"I understand, sir."

Coach makes an exasperated sound. "Do you even care about this?"

I care about a lot of things, but I'm not sure hockey is one of them anymore. Keeping those thoughts to myself, I give him the answer he's expecting. "Yes, of course I do."

His eyes sink closed, and he inhales slowly. "The team is suspending you."

My stomach twists as I meet his eyes, waiting for my punishment.

"For eight games."

Damn. It's more serious than I expected. But I did blindside Raduloff, and he could have been seriously injured. He's on concussion protocol now. Because of me.

"And before you can return, we require that you speak to someone."

"Speak to someone?" I glance over at the lady the league sent over.

Distractedly, he nods. "Yes. we requiring you to work with a therapist and they will sign off on your suitability to return once they're satisfied that you have your anger, frustrations, or whatever it is sorted out. Because what happened yesterday can't happen again."

Fuck.

Talking about feelings isn't my strong point. I certainly don't need anger management, or any kind of therapy. I just need a second to fucking breathe.

I haven't even begun to process the gaping hole my father's sudden death has left in my life. He died just as the season started, so I couldn't fall apart then. I told myself I'd deal with it, just not yet.

Not only am I trying to come to terms with losing my dad, but I also feel guilty that my mother and brothers need me back home in Colorado. But Mom insisted that I stay in Boston, playing hockey like my dad would have wanted.

I look up, realizing Coach is still waiting for my response.

My mouth is dry, but I don't dare ask him for a bottle of water. I'm not exactly in a position to be asking for favors right now, no matter how small.

"Okay," I hear myself say, because what other choice do I have?

Wilder hands me a sheet of paper. "These are the approved sports therapists. Pick one and set up the appointment. Sooner rather than later."

"Sure," I manage to say.

"The league doesn't tolerate this kind of shit, kid. Not anymore. The ice isn't the place for some frat-party brawl. It's your workplace, and you're not getting the job done. When you don't get the job done, we have to make tough decisions. Do you hear what I'm saying?"

I take a deep breath, trying to get my breathing

under control. I understand exactly what he's saying. They're close to ripping up my multimillion-dollar contract if I don't get my shit sorted out.

"Yes, sir." I swallow and hold out my hand. "I understand what you're saying."

2

SUMMER

I step out onto the tarmac where the plane waits in the distance. Shouldering my bag, I get in line, shivering in the cold air. It looks like it's going to snow, and I'm not really dressed for it. It's only October. Instead of snow boots and a thick coat, I'm wearing high-heeled ankle boots and a too-thin jacket, but at least I thought to bring mittens.

I flew from Boston to Denver this morning, and now I'm about to board a second flight to Durango. Then I'll take a shuttle to Lost Haven, population six hundred eight. I've never been to a town so small. Didn't even realize places like that still exist.

"Hello?" I murmur after pulling my phone out of my jacket.

"Summer? Is that you?"

"Yes. It's me. Bad connection? I'm getting ready to get onto my second flight."

"No, I can hear you now. I'm glad I reached you. I've got some intel."

"Great. What have you got for me, Les?"

Les has been a mentor to me in a lot of ways. He manages the front office of the Boston Titans hockey team, and I interned for him when I was still in college, studying sports management. He was the one who got me this job—which is to track down a promising rookie who's trying to blow his entire season by fighting everyone who looks at him the wrong way.

Logan was suspended for eight games and has to get the written approval of a therapist before he can return. I'm one of three team-approved therapists. But Logan isn't returning my phone calls, and he's yet to make a decision on a therapist.

So, here I am. On the other side of the country, chasing down a rogue rookie with an anger-management problem. I guess this is my life now.

"Logan is definitely there," Les says. "He arrived yesterday, but no one on the team has been able to reach him."

"Thank you. I'll be there by late afternoon. I'll see what I can do."

"You clinch this one, kid, and you'll have it made."

I don't know about that, but if I succeed, at least I'll be able to make my rent next month.

"I sent you over an email with everything in his file. It's not much."

"I'm sure it'll help. Thanks, Les."

He chuckles. "You haven't met Logan yet. You're going to need all the help you can get."

Logan Tate is a twenty-three-year-old rookie defenseman who was signed to the Titans last year for $2.6 million, but I don't really know much about him. What I do know is that he's six foot two, one hundred ninety-five pounds, and built like a bull—all muscle and brawn. I watched a few of his clips online. His speed was impressive.

I also learned that Logan lost his father unexpectedly this summer, and has had some family turmoil that's distracting him from the game. The gossip sites have plenty of compromising photos of him leaving various bars and clubs at all hours of the night. And he got into three fights in his first two games of the season, one of which was with his own teammate. The final straw was a major penalty for misconduct against a player from the Avalanche.

All of this bad publicity doesn't look good on a rookie, especially a high-priced newcomer with a lot of unproven talent. The organization is ready to release him, and they will if I can't get through to him.

But if I do? There's a nice paycheck waiting for me. Not to mention the credibility it will bring to my business. And that's why I decided to track him down, which led me to his family's property in the mountains of Colorado.

"Has he been in counseling before?" I adjust the strap of my overnight bag on my shoulder and climb the stairs to board the plane.

"Nope. Not to my knowledge," Les says. "Unless you count the intake interview all players are required to complete prior to signing the contract. It's all in the file. Very standard stuff. As a defenseman, he has strong protective instincts. But his assessments showed him to be a team player, which is why his behavior on the ice is so strange and very unexpected."

"Gotcha. Well, that's a positive."

I board the plane, ignoring the annoyed look

from the stewardess as I take my seat in the third row of the tiny aircraft and push down an uneasy feeling.

"So, what's your plan?" Les asks as I buckle my seat belt and settle in.

"That's easy. Find Lost Haven, fix your broken hockey player, and get the heck out of here before the snow arrives."

Les made a mocking sound. "You make it sound so easy."

I have no choice but to succeed. I have student loans out the wazoo, and no fallback plans.

Another annoyed look from the flight attendant prompts me to say my good-byes to Les.

"See you soon," I say, confident I'll be back in Boston before the end of the week.

• • •

The scene painted before me is like a postcard, and I take it all in as the shuttle van carries me through Lost Haven.

Towering pine trees surround me, and a winding river runs alongside the gravel road that winds through a canyon carved between two mountain ranges. The air smells like pine needles, and the sky is a bright robin's egg blue. It's breathtaking, and I drink in every detail. This may very well be the most beautiful place I've ever visited, and I can't ignore the little voice in my head whispering that I wish there were more time to explore.

"Are we almost there?" I ask.

The driver nods. "Just about."

I inhale, silently practicing the speech I rehearsed on the last flight. Logan may be resistant, but given that I'm his ticket back into the game he loves, I'm not anticipating much of a challenge.

The van slows as the driver turns onto yet another long gravel road with thick trees lining both sides of it. It's not until a house comes into view that I realize it's not a road, but a driveway. A very long and winding driveway.

When the van stops in front of the house, I'm hit by a sudden wave of nerves.

Hunting down a potential client like this isn't something I've ever done. To be honest, it's unheard of. But between Logan refusing to return my phone calls and emails, and Les telling me about how much this player needs the help . . . I'm here. And let's not forget what this opportunity can do for my career

Nerves may be filling my stomach, but I'm here, and I know a thing or two about pretending you have it all together, even when you don't. I'm not going to focus on the fact that I may be violating a professional code of conduct by showing up like this. Honestly, if I'd known just how remote this place was, I'm not sure I would have come at all. I didn't see a single motel on the hour-long drive up the mountain. But I'll deal with that once I've pitched my services to Logan. At least I've still got some daylight left to figure things out before night falls.

The driver hands me my bags—a laptop case and a leather duffel bag—while I shoulder my oversized purse.

"Good luck. Stay warm," he says, grinning at my thin jacket.

"Thanks for the ride."

He nods once and climbs back inside.

Well, here goes nothing.

The van pulls away, leaving me alone in front of the house. I feel so small under the enormous trees and endless expanse of sky.

As I approach the house, I take note of the details. It's cheery looking, two stories with bluish-gray siding and fieldstone accents. Cedar pillars flank the stone porch. Shutters are in need of a new coat of paint. A potted juniper sits to the left of the large front door.

Before I can reach the door, it opens, and a middle-aged woman with shoulder-length hair and kind blue eyes steps out.

"Can I help you, honey? Are you lost?"

I straighten my shoulders and extend my hand. "I'm Summer Campbell. The team sent me." *Sort of.* "I'm looking for Logan."

She gently shakes my hand, breaking into a smile. "Oh, come on in then. He's inside warming up."

Without anything further, she leads me inside. The foyer is large, with storage for coats and boots, and I set my bags on a bench before following her. The living room is warm and inviting with a large fireplace lit with a cozy fire. The windows look out onto endless green, and the whole house smells faintly of damp wool and cinnamon.

An older man with a gray beard rests in a recliner in front of the fireplace, reading a newspaper.

"Forgive me. I'm Jillian, Logan's mother. And

this is Grandpa Al." She gestures to the man.

He lifts his head to get a look at me. "Albert Tate. Nice to meet you. Jillian, offer the lady something to drink." His voice is gruff, but there's a tenderness to him too.

"Oh yes, how rude of me." Jillian touches her cheek, then looks toward the other room. "Logan, Summer's here to see you," she calls out.

A man is standing in the dining room watching us, and I don't know how I didn't notice him before. He's very tall, and well, he's . . . enormous. His T-shirt hugs his biceps, which are huge and muscular. His dark brown hair is rumpled, possibly from the knit hat he holds in one hand. His eyes are blue, like his mother's, but with none of the same kindness.

When he takes a step closer, a spike of something hot and unfamiliar races through me. I've never been attracted to a potential client before, and it's disorienting.

"Hi, um, Logan. I'm Summer, a sports psychologist." I gesture to myself.

His eyes narrow and his jaw tightens. Apparently, I'm not off to a great start.

I try to smile, but I fear it looks less inviting

and more calculating. "Can we talk for a minute?"

"I don't have anything to say to you," he says in a deep voice that causes my stomach to jump.

Weird. That's never happened before.

I clear my throat. "I'm . . . *sorry*? Your season is hanging in the balance, and—"

He stalks closer. "Actually, I do have something to say. Did you follow me all the way here from Boston?"

"Follow you? Um . . . no." I glance at Jillian, who's smiling nervously at me. I clear my throat. "I came here to help you get back on the ice. And since you weren't returning my calls or emails . . ."

My surprise at his willingness to just outright refuse my help must be written all over my face. Inhaling sharply, I turn toward his mother for reinforcements.

"How about some tea? Can I get you some tea, Summer?" Jillian asks sweetly.

"No tea," Logan says, his voice a deep rumble. "She's not staying."

"That's crazy," Jillian says, scolding her son. "She came all the way here. Let the girl warm up and at least hear what she has to say."

I'm liking her more and more.

Logan exhales, a muscle jumping in his jaw. "Fine. You have five minutes."

Turning back to me, Jillian grins. "Great. Would you like chamomile or English breakfast? I have coffee too."

"I'm fine," I say, waving off her hospitality.

"Get her one of those cinnamon buns with her coffee, Jill," Grandpa Al calls out from his armchair.

"Okay, that would be lovely," I say cautiously, giving her a grateful smile. At the mention of food, my grumbling stomach reminds me that I haven't eaten since breakfast, which was an awful breakfast burrito at the airport that I only managed a few bites of. It hardly counts as breakfast.

I'm sensing that while Logan might not want me here, his mother and grandfather seem to understand my presence here is important for his future. I guess that's one tick in the plus column.

Taking a deep breath, I follow Jillian to the kitchen. She gestures for me to take a seat at the table while she retrieves a mug from the cabinet. I follow her instructions, pulling out a sturdy wooden chair and sitting down.

The kitchen is large with plenty of cabinets, all painted in a soft gray color. Healthy plants fill the window box, and there's a big bowl of fruit on the table, along with a half-finished puzzle. It's a family home—the kind I always dreamed about while growing up, but never got to experience. Complete with creaky wooden floors and books overflowing from the bookcases.

I ramble when I'm nervous, so it's no surprise that I begin filling the empty silence with nonsensical chatter. "It's a lovely property you have here. So serene."

"Cream or sugar, honey?" Jillian asks, holding up the coffee carafe.

"Both, please."

As she pours me a coffee, Logan wanders in and leans against the doorway, appraising us. His cool, indifferent gaze makes me nervous.

Jillian places a steaming mug of coffee before me and sits down. Folding her hands on the table before her, she meets my eyes. "So, you were saying you're a sports . . ."

"Psychologist, yes." I take a sip of my coffee.

People get nervous when they hear that word, but they shouldn't. I'm as non-threatening as they come. I mean . . . if they only knew. My own life is kind of a dumpster fire at the moment. But I doubt that's what they want to hear, so instead, I launch into my backstory.

"After graduating with a bachelor's degree in sports medicine, I interned for Les—um, Les Benson, he works for the Titans." I look to Logan, because surely he knows who Les is, but he looks completely disinterested. "Anyway, I worked for him while getting my master's degree in psychology. And after I graduated and started working with athletes, I quickly learned that stretching and taping sore muscles wasn't going to fix their injuries, when a lot of them ran much deeper than that."

Jillian is nodding along, but Logan hasn't said anything else. So I just continue.

"Sometimes they need things a physical therapist can't provide. Like counseling, or someone to talk to. Help dealing with performance anxiety. Or overcoming obstacles to improve their performance. A lot of times those things are mental, not physical."

I pause for a moment, letting my words sink in. I'm guessing this may describe Logan, because by all appearances, he looks normal and healthy.

"Anyway, all of this made me want to start my

own business, so I did, shortly after graduating."

Jillian's mouth tilts up in a smile.

It may sound impressive that I started my own company, but it's tricky. I need to win over clients—*paying* clients—if I want to succeed and keep a roof over my head. Now that I have this opportunity, I refuse to blow it. I didn't fly across the country to fail. If I can get him back out on the ice, scoring goals, it will go a long way toward building my professional reputation.

Logan still stands glowering at me in the doorway, his back ramrod straight, not saying a word.

I'm off to a stellar start.

God help me.

3

LOGAN

Nothing in my life makes sense anymore, not since Dad died. And now being home, seeing the worry lines on my mom's face, and how much slower Grandpa is at getting around, hockey is the furthest thing from my mind.

And this chick . . . Summer with her sharp tongue and inquisitive eyes, thinks she can just stroll in here and fix me? Not a chance.

Summer and my mom have been chatting for the past forty minutes, so I wandered outside to check on the firewood situation behind the shed, wanting to clear my head. It does fuck-all to help. Maybe if I hadn't been so blindsided by this . . . maybe if she wasn't a complete babe, I'd have a shot at acting somewhat normal. Instead, I'm acting like a dick.

But, hey . . . I guess that's what I do best these days.

And what did anyone expect? I can't be forced into talking about my feelings with a complete stranger. Especially not someone my own mother gave the last cinnamon bun to. I mean, *fuck*.

My season has been doomed from the start, and now that I'm here, the idea of leaving again has me feeling more uncertain than ever about what I want my future to look like. And while it's true that I've had anger issues since my dad died, and there's family turmoil, I highly doubt Summer is going to be the one to help me.

The fact is, it's hard being a thousand miles away trying to play hockey when you can't get your head in the game because you're constantly worried about what's going on back home. How is she going to fix that? Wave a magic wand and make everything right in my world? Come on, life just doesn't work that way.

When I walk back inside, Grandpa Al has joined them in the kitchen. He's helped himself to a slice of brisket left over from lunch, which won't be good for his cholesterol, but you try telling him that. And he's laughing at some story Summer is telling them.

"Unless you count a really stubborn racoon last summer, no, no roommates," she says with a smile.

Grandpa Al chuckles, and even Mom seems too enamored with Summer to scold him for stealing a slice of the leftover brisket.

My mom pats Summer's hand before her gaze lifts to mine. "Logan, will you set up Summer in the Evergreen cabin?"

I stiffen. She can't be serious. "A word, Mother?"

Mom follows me into the living room, her brow knit with confusion. "Just hear her out, honey," she says soothingly.

"Whose side are you on?"

"There's no sides here."

My life is sports. There are always sides.

"She can't stay here," I hiss, keeping my voice low.

"Why on earth not? She's offering to help you, and as far as I can tell, you need the help. Do not blow this. Plus, have you seen the girl? She's gorgeous, and she's really sweet. I like her."

"*Mother.*"

"Well, she is." Mom plants her hands on her hips.

"Don't meddle in the boy's affairs, Jillian," Grandpa Al calls from the kitchen.

I knew they could hear us. Damn house isn't big enough.

"Thanks, Gramps," I say with a defeated sigh, heading back into the kitchen as Mom trails behind me again.

"Anytime, kid." He grins at me. "You just get better so you can get out on the ice again. And speaking of . . . I still haven't gotten those hockey tickets you promised me."

"You can't fly, Al. It's bad for your blood pressure," Mom says, scolding him.

My gaze drops to Summer, and she shifts uncomfortably in her seat. Maybe she isn't used to family drama. Maybe her own family is comprised of perfectly normal people who don't constantly argue and meddle in one another's lives. I have no idea what that would be like.

Seeming to sense her discomfort, Mom gives me another stern look before putting a comforting hand on Summer's shoulder. "We're going to get you set up in the cabin. Don't ever let it be said that the Tates aren't hospitable."

"Thank you. That's very generous of you," Summer says, her gaze shooting to me to read my reaction. Which is less than enthusiastic.

"Dinner will be at six, honey," Mom adds.

Summer shakes her head. "Oh, thank you, but you don't have to . . ."

"Oh yes I do. In case you haven't noticed, there aren't any restaurants or take-out places nearby. And the cabin's kitchenette is basically just a kettle and a hot plate."

Summer fidgets nervously before rising to her feet. "Okay then. If you insist."

"I do. And it'll give me the chance to grill you about where you got that adorable scarf."

Summer smiles. And then everyone is silent.

Why is this so awkward? Why did she come here?

"Ahem." Mom stands there glaring at me.

"I'll show you the cabin," I mutter begrudgingly.

Mom's grimace turns into a smile. Nothing makes her happier than good manners.

I shove one hand in my pocket and look over to Summer. "Ready?"

"Sure," she says with a nod. "After you."

In the foyer, I shoulder her bag. She must not have packed very much, which bodes well for me, because hopefully that means she won't be here for long.

We start along the path toward the back of the property where two cabins sit at the river's edge. Our boots crunch on the fallen pine needles on the walking path. It's already gotten cold this fall, and there's an early snow in the forecast later this week.

"Those the only shoes you have?" I ask, noticing the high heels on her boots.

"Yeah."

I shake my head. "And your only coat?"

"What?" she says, blinking at me with an annoyed look. "How could I know you'd live on the side of a mountain in the middle of a dang forest?"

I smirk. Her choice in footwear told me that much. "Fair point."

I guess it was pretty ballsy of her following me out here.

"So . . . you're from Colorado originally?" she

asks, her voice pleasant and hopeful.

"You shouldn't have come here," I say, ignoring her question.

Summer's steps falter, but only for a second. "Do you always say exactly what you're thinking?"

My gaze jumps to hers briefly. "Nope. Never, actually."

Summer hurries along beside me, her long legs working to keep up with me. "If I can work with you, it will mean everything for my business."

I stop abruptly, facing her with a scowl. "You want to fix me? I'm not a broken toy you can piece back together."

Summer nods. "That's exactly what you are. You're a very valuable asset to the Titans organization, and they need you pieced back together. If you're serious about your career and want to get back on the ice, this is your chance, so why not let me help you?"

I inhale sharply but don't say anything else. My struggles are no one's business but mine, and I want to keep it that way.

We reach the cabin in silence, and I pull open its door and test the lights. Everything looks normal. She might have roomed with a raccoon before, but I doubt she'd want to tonight.

I set her bag on the porch and give her a nod. "See you at dinner. Don't be late."

Then I turn and head back toward the house, developing a new plan with each step I take.

I'll just have to set my attraction to her aside. She can't stay here. And I'm going to see to that.

4

SUMMER

After spending a chilly night alone in the cabin, I dig through my duffel bag, looking for something warm to wear. A dusting of snow has fallen overnight and I'm sure the temperature has dropped. I settle on a warm fleece sweater and jeans, and then pull my hair into a low ponytail.

Last evening, I went up to the house at six and had dinner with Jillian, Grandpa Al, and Logan's oldest brother, Graham. Logan wasn't there, and no one said a word about him.

Jillian tried to be accommodating by bringing me into the conversation and making me feel welcome, but I still felt awkward about the entire thing. After dinner, I helped by loading the dishwasher, not wanting to eat and run, but then I got the heck out of there and disappeared into the cabin.

Les called, but I let it go to voice mail, too chicken to answer. I didn't want him to know that I was hiding out in some remote cabin alone all night long because Logan refused to speak to me. I don't do well with failure, but there was little I could do if Logan flat-out refused and disappeared into thin air.

I spent the rest of the evening bundled up in the cabin's double bed, reading over the files Les had sent me. Unfortunately, they weren't much help.

Logan was an active and reliable member of the team last season. This past summer, his father died unexpectedly, and Logan went home for a few weeks to attend the funeral and be with his family. He returned to Boston in time for training camp and performed well, so it was a shock to the team, its owner, and the coaches that he'd struggle going into the season. Those struggles led to his current and very serious suspension.

Deciding that I'm in desperate need of coffee to help warm up, I put on my jacket and head up to the house. I figure if I'm going to gain Logan's trust, a little family recon might be necessary.

Graham only said about three words the entire evening, but Jillian and Grandpa Al are both fairly chatty. I learned that the Tate clan is bigger than I realized. After Graham came Austen, Matt, and then Logan. Apparently all three older brothers live on the property. Logan was the only one who moved away—to pursue his dream of playing hockey—but now I wonder if he feels guilty about that. With his dad gone and the rest of his family left here to run things… It's something I'll try to get to the bottom of while I'm here.

When I reach the house and let myself inside, I'm immediately struck by the volume of noise coming from the kitchen. It's so different from the almost eerily silent evening I spent alone in my cabin. The sound of arguing, of loud male laughter, and someone shouting about whoever took the last cup of coffee, echoes through the house.

I pause by the door and almost consider fleeing. But that's not me. I don't run from challenging situations. I can do this. So I stand up taller and remove my jacket, hanging it with my scarf on a hook in the foyer.

The first thing I notice is how much smaller the kitchen seems today. It's filled with bodies. Large male bodies. Jillian shoos someone away from the counter with a kitchen towel.

"Oh, Summer, there you are. I was worried we'd have to send a search party out into the woods."

"Good morning," I say, noticing that Logan is seated in the formal dining room with his grandfather.

I'm introduced to Austen—who seems quiet and observant, and Matt—who looks most similar to Logan, though he offers me a warm smile. Graham quietly focuses on his breakfast, a big plate of fried eggs and several strips of bacon.

Graham is even more stoic than he was last night. He's taller than the others by maybe an inch or so. But all four of the Tate brothers share a lot of the same features. They're broad and muscular with dark hair and darker stubble. Bright blue eyes framed by thick eyelashes and big, rugged hands.

"I'm making another pot of coffee. Give me two minutes," Jillian says, dumping coffee beans into a countertop grinder.

I nod. "Anything I can do?"

Jillian presses the button on the grinder, and it whirs to life. She shakes her head in response to my offer for help.

My gaze roams the kitchen. The breakfast table has been turned into a pastry station. It's covered in flour, and a large lump of dough and a rolling pin are sitting there waiting for Jillian's return.

I make myself useful and begin drying dishes so that I don't do something incredibly stupid like ogle all four brothers. It's already embarrassing enough how much Logan's presence seems to affect me. My stomach tingles with nerves, and my hands feel clammy every time I'm around him.

In the adjoining dining room, the breakfast conversation is *loud*.

With wide eyes, I take in the scene before me. There's arguing, and laughing, and bacon being stolen from a plate, and one brother slapping another upside the head . . . it's *a lot* different from what I'm used to as an only child. My life is quiet, and so to be thrust into the middle of this is a little disorienting.

"Austen, grab the lady a chair, would you," Grandpa Al says from the other end of the table.

Austen hops up, momentarily abandoning his own plate of eggs to fetch me a chair from the breakfast table, and carries it over to the larger dining table. He sets it down next to Logan, who still hasn't acknowledged my presence. *Okay, that's awkward.*

Standing uncomfortably in the doorway, I'm not sure how to feel, but I shoot Grandpa Al a grateful look. He stabs a sausage link with his fork and goes right back to his breakfast.

Jillian steers me by the shoulders toward the breakfast table. "Sit. Eat something." She places a mug of coffee in front of me.

I open my mouth to protest, but she shakes her head with a firm look. "You've done enough already. Besides, we can't spoil these boys too much, or they'll never leave my house and go off and find themselves wives."

At this, Matt, who's seated beside me, chuckles. "I'm not in the market for a wife, Mom."

"And how could you be when they all leave your bed after one night?" Austen says with an eye roll.

Matt grins and lifts one shoulder in a shrug. "Plenty of satisfied customers, though."

"For goodness' sake, behave, boys," Jillian says, handing me a clean plate.

I fill it with two strips of bacon and a blueberry scone.

"A truly satisfied customer would be a *repeat* customer," Grandpa Al says from one end of the table.

When it dawns on me that he's teasing his

grandson about basically being a hit-it-and-quit-it player, inappropriate laughter bursts from my lips.

Jillian pats my shoulder. "Don't encourage him, dear."

I press my lips together.

Finished with his breakfast, Graham pushes his empty plate away and leans his elbows on the table. "If you morons are done arguing, we have things to discuss. There's lots on the agenda today."

"Yes, boss," Matt says with a groan.

I nibble on my scone and listen to the day's plans.

"The Polaris needs spark plugs, and the shed needs re-roofing before the snow flies. Plus, I need help with the beer-brewing process today."

"The beer's not ready," Matt says. "So, what do you need help with?"

"Someone's got to babysit the fermentation process, and I can't be in two places at once," Graham says gruffly.

Logan looks up from his plate. "I'll help out. Wherever you need me."

I venture a look in his direction. I know I don't belong here, but I won't do well with being ignored all day either. "Can I speak to you after breakfast?"

He meets my eyes for the first time today, and a shock of awareness buzzes through me. "Sure. Once I help Austen in the garage."

"Okay," I say with a nod.

After a few minutes sorting out who will be working where today, the guys rise from the table, clearing plates and pausing to lean over to give their mom a quick peek on the cheek, thanking her for breakfast. Even Graham.

"Thanks for feeding us, Mom," he says, stacking his plate with the others by the sink.

"You need more coffee?" she asks.

"I'd better not."

Once they've left out the back door, the house goes quiet. Grandpa Al retires to the living room and settles into his recliner with a newspaper.

I busy myself by rinsing dishes and loading them into the dishwasher while Jillian cleans her cast iron skillet. Now that we're alone, I recognize that this is my opportunity.

"Jillian?"

"Hmm?" She wipes the skillet dry and places it in a cabinet.

"I know we just met and all, but I just wanted to say how sorry I was to hear about the passing of your husband last summer."

She gives me a warm look. "Thank you, honey. Thirty-two years, we were married. I loved him with my whole heart," she says with a faraway look in her eyes that pinches my heart.

"That must have been hard on all of you."

"It was. Hardest damn time in my life. Some of the boys took it harder than others."

"Like Logan?" I ask, rinsing a mixing bowl.

Jillian's about to respond when footsteps draw our attention.

Logan is standing in the kitchen doorway, wearing a look of fury.

He overheard everything.

Shit.

And he does *not* look happy.

5

LOGAN

Forget. This.

Furious, I storm out the back door with Summer hot on my trail.

"Logan, wait!" she calls out after me.

But I don't wait. I don't even slow down.

Summer's been here for less than twenty-four fucking hours, and she's already talking about me with my mother. If that's not an invasion of privacy, I don't know what the hell is. I should have kicked her out on her ass yesterday because she has no right to be here.

And now she's pretending like she cares about me and the family, and bringing up my father? Fuck that. She doesn't care about me or this family, despite what she wants my mom to believe. This is her *job*.

"Please, let me explain," Summer calls out. "I'm sorry I brought things up with your mom."

Scowling, I turn and face her, waiting for her to catch up. "This isn't going to work. You need to pack up your shit and go back to Boston. You don't belong here."

"Logan, please. I was serious when I said I wanted to help you."

"Yeah?" I scoff. "I don't see how it's going to help me to have some psychologist dredging up the past and talking to my family about me."

She chews on her lip and looks down at the ground for a moment before meeting my eyes again. "I know what it's like to lose someone, so I have some kind of idea of how you might be feeling."

It's not what I expected her to say, and for a moment, I'm speechless. "Who?"

"My mom," she says quietly. "She was my best friend. Her death devastated me and still does."

My stomach tightens, and I swallow the sour taste of regret. "Look, I'm sorry. I didn't know."

Summer nods. "It's not something I announce

when I meet new people."

"How long ago?" My tone has softened significantly, and when Summer looks up, she gives me a small, sad smile.

"Two years." She swallows and takes a breath. "But sometimes it feels like so much longer. I can barely remember her laugh, and I hate that. It kills me."

A pang of emotion wells inside me. "What about your dad?" I ask, suddenly more interested than I wish I were. She's supposed to be packing and leaving, but instead I'm asking about her family. And I have no idea why.

"I never knew him."

"Siblings?"

She shakes her head. "I'm an only child. It was only ever me and Mom."

"Shit. I'm sorry."

It's in this moment that I realize I've been acting like an asshole. Just because I'm mad about, well, *everything*, it doesn't make it okay to take it out on her.

But Summer is an easy target. A stranger. Someone I plan on never seeing again. But even though I may not know her, I can't help hating the thought that she's alone in this world without any family.

"So, breakfast must have been a whole new experience for you then." I smile, nodding back toward the house where my loud-ass family probably frightened her.

"It was very eye-opening," she says with a chuckle. "But in a good way. I've never experienced that. Never had a big family. And now it's just me."

Even if I've felt lost and out of control lately, her words remind me that I'm a lot more fortunate than most. I have a family, people I can count on and who'll support me through the shitstorm currently facing us. Still, that doesn't mean everything is magically going to be okay, and that's what I'm struggling with.

How's life ever supposed to be "normal" again?

"They love you, you know," Summer says softly. "They just want you to be okay."

I nod. "I know." When the wind picks up and Summer wraps her arms around herself, I say, "Come on. I'll walk you back to your cabin."

It's about a hundred yards from the house, and

we're quiet most of the way. When we get there, Summer opens the door and pauses in the entry-way.

"So, after you help Austen in the garage . . ."

I peer around her, realizing the woodburning stove is empty and the place feels cold. "Did you start a fire last night?"

She looks over her shoulder at the stove. "No. I don't know how. City-girl problems." She shrugs.

Shit. "You must have been freezing last night."

She gives me a sheepish look. "Yeah. I slept in my coat and scarf. I figured you guys were crazy living out here like this."

"Well, we might be crazy, but we don't have to sleep in our coats." I gesture to the woodstove. "May I?"

"Oh my goodness, please do." She steps aside and ushers me in with a wave of her hand.

I came here to force her to leave after I cussed her out.

Now I'm offering to make her comfortable and warm.

6

SUMMER

"I have an idea," I say after following Logan into the small cabin. "What if we just be honest with each other?"

He stops and glances over his shoulder at me. "What's that supposed to mean? You think I'm going to lie to you?"

"No. Definitely not. But I do think that as humans, we have a tendency to gloss over the tough subjects to avoid showing our true emotions."

His brows lift. "Gloss?" Disdain drips off the word—like he's suddenly assessing me and wondering if I'm some new-age, voodoo-loving therapist.

I chuckle, shaking my head. "*Gloss*. To give off a superficially attractive appearance or impression."

"Right." Logan scratches at the stubble on his chin, and then nods. "I guess that's true."

"So, all I'm saying is, what if we don't do that with each other?"

"What are you proposing? Total honesty?" He scoffs, although his gaze doesn't leave mine. As if he's considering my proposal.

I nod. "Total honesty. Both ways. You be totally honest with me, and I'll be totally honest with you."

He turns toward a bin and inspects the wood situation. Without a word, he walks past me and disappears outside.

I suck in a deep breath, silently cursing myself. Have I pushed him too far, too soon?

I'm about to follow him outside, when he reappears carrying a stack of firewood. After dropping the wood into the bin, he turns toward me.

"If honesty's what you want, I can try. But I can't promise anything. I'm not a *share your feelings* kinda guy, and I doubt I ever will be."

He's still watching me. Having Logan's full attention is almost dizzying. He's intense and electrifying, all rolled into one. He's also huge and muscular and gorgeous…

"I'll, uh, go first," I stammer, trying to be a professional instead of a woman who's noticing how very attractive this man is.

Get it together, Summer.

I need to show Logan that he can trust me, and one way of showing him that is by sharing my deepest thoughts and secrets. But then I hesitate, because I'm suddenly a little self-conscious about the truth-bomb I'm about to drop on him. It's been a constant thought I've had since I got here. Maybe part of me is desperate to admit this out loud to another human being.

After swallowing hard, I begin. "I'm alone a lot, and it scares me how much I've gotten used to that. Seeing your family here and being around them, seeing how much they all rely on one another and generally need one another . . . I'm scared I'll never have that. And it petrifies me that I'm going to be alone forever with no one or no family to call my own."

When Logan doesn't say anything for several heartbeats, I grow self-conscious and focus on the floor. "Too much *total honesty* for you?"

He shakes his head. "No. Not at all. You . . .

live alone?"

"Yes. I have a studio apartment. Four hundred fifty square feet, all to myself."

He curses under his breath, looking surprised. "I've stayed in bigger hotel rooms."

Sighing, I nod. "So have I."

I don't need to tell him it's all I can afford. I'm sure he's aware that his salary and mine are miles apart, and that Boston is an extremely expensive city to live in.

Chewing on my lip, I hesitate briefly before asking, "What about you?"

"You want total honesty?" His voice carries a touch of uncertainty.

I nod, wondering if I'm eager for his answer because I'm a therapist, or because I'm a human looking for connection with a stranger.

Like me, he hesitates, and I wonder if he's going to tell me something at all. Or maybe he'll decide against the whole honesty thing. If he refuses, I'm not sure what comes next.

"I'm glad I wasn't here," he says softly, like he's letting me in on a secret. "When my father died. I'm glad I wasn't here."

I glance over at him, disbelief surely written across my features.

"I know that sounds fucking awful, because if I'd been here, I could have spent time with him. Could have had one last visit with him before he was gone. But on the other hand, if I'd been here, I don't think I would have handled it very well. Watching my mother and brothers fall apart . . . watching him be whisked away in an ambulance without being able to do anything to help him. Is it crazy if I say I'm happy that those aren't my last memories of my dad?"

I find my voice. "It's not crazy. And part of me understands that completely."

He gives me a quick glance to check my reaction. Surely, he can see that I'm sincere. I don't judge him at all for this admission.

"Your turn."

"Total honesty?" I ask.

I guess this is our new thing—this little catchphrase before we say something we wouldn't otherwise admit to a total stranger. Why does this feel so much harder than I thought it would? My heart is beating fast, and my hands feel shaky.

Logan nods to encourage me, giving me a reassuring look, but I'm still uncertain if I should really share what's lingering on the tip of my tongue. He's probably going to think I'm a monster.

I take a deep breath, then give him my truth. "I paid someone to deliver my mother's eulogy."

"What? Why?" The words leave his lips in a rush, and he stands up straight, forgetting about starting the fire and concentrating entirely on me.

I smile gently. "Because I knew I wouldn't be able to deliver it myself. I was a mess, barely able to function, so I knew there was no way I could stand in front of people and speak. And my mom's best friend felt the same. There was no one else but us, and I couldn't stomach the idea that no one would stand up for Mom and talk about the amazing woman she was, about the incredible and selfless life she'd lived."

Swallowing hard, I gather my composure. It was such a difficult and dark time. I give myself a moment to draw a few steadying breaths as flashbacks slam into me.

"I found this website where you can hire someone for a small fee, and I paid seventy-five dollars to a woman who was well-versed in public speaking."

Logan lays a hand on my shoulder and gives it

a light squeeze. It's the first time he's touched me. I'm sure he doesn't mean it to be anything more than a comforting gesture, but a sudden flash of heat passes between us at his touch.

Can he feel it too?

Warmth rushes from my shoulder and settles in my chest. Unexpected emotion wells inside me. It's been so long since anyone has touched me. I'm sure that's the only reason why his touch affects me so much. It can't be anything else.

When he removes his hand a second later, I pull in a breath, urging myself to continue. "And as I sat there listening to her read the words I'd written, I felt ashamed."

"Why?" Logan asks, looking genuinely perplexed.

I shrug. "I don't know. Just like I had lied or something."

He meets my eyes, and there's a newfound understanding between us. "It wasn't a lie, Summer. I think it was really nice what you did."

"Thanks. I appreciate that." I smile.

We stare at each other for a beat too long before his gaze darts away and his body becomes rigid again. It's as if he's remembered why I'm here.

Up go his walls, and I feel like I'll have to begin to chip away at them all over again.

7

LOGAN

After the weighty discussion we've just had, the air around us is tense, but there's also a sense of calm and healing that I haven't felt in a long time. I shake out of my daze and refocus on the fire that I've yet to start.

"Give me a few minutes, and I'll get this going."

As I load the woodstove with kindling, I focus on the task at hand and allow myself to clear my head of thoughts of how easy it felt to tell Summer things I've never told anyone. Admitting that I was glad I wasn't here when Dad died . . . I never thought I'd ever say that out loud to anyone.

But I can't say I regret it either. There was something kinda freeing in admitting that.

The kindling catches, and the first crackle of fire licking at the logs makes Summer hum happily to herself. The temperature is only in the forties. I can't imagine how cold she must have been in here last night.

All the animosity I felt earlier overhearing her gossip with my mom is gone. Summer is here to do a job, and I haven't made it easy on her. I've been an asshole. Simple as that.

Stacking more wood in the fire with some paper, I say, "Tell me about your mom. What was she like?"

When I glance at Summer, she has a faraway look in her eyes. "She was spunky and fun, not at all one of those helicopter parents. She never hovered. She let me figure things out, but I knew she'd be there if and when I needed her."

"That's cool."

Summer nods. "She was."

When I close the door to the stove, I feel Summer behind me. "Do you want me to show you how to get this started again if it goes out?"

She nods. "Yeah, that would be helpful."

"So, you want to get the kindling just right. That part's important."

I show her how to add more logs. Summer's quiet while I mess with it. Once I'm done, I close the door to the stove again.

"That should last you about two hours. Just keep adding more wood."

She stands in front of the stove, rubbing her hands together in the warmth it's slowly starting to put off.

"Better?" I ask, standing to join her.

"So much better." She smiles. "I'm happy I won't have to wear twenty layers to bed tonight."

Another punch of emotion hits me right in the chest.

Summer is so cheerful and good-tempered, even when I've been nothing but a dick to her. Even when she doesn't have any family left in the world. Even when she nearly froze to death, sleeping in her jacket last night. It's like nothing fazes her. She's still smiling.

Who is this girl?

For the first time in a long time, I find I want to spend time getting to know a woman. Part of me wishes she'd be here long enough for me to figure out who Summer Campbell truly is.

"Did you grow up here on the property?" she asks, changing the topic back to me.

"No, we only moved here about ten years ago. I was thirteen. We lived in a town a couple of hours away before this. But this was my dad's dream, living off the land as much as possible. Space to roam, and space for us to just be kids."

Summer nods. "It's a nice dream to have."

I raise one shoulder. "It can be. It can also be a difficult one." As is evidenced by how much Graham is struggling to get things to work.

"Will you tell me about him?" she asks, her expression growing soft.

"My dad?"

She nods.

I'm not sure I want to, but then before I decide to keep quiet, words start to spill out of me. "He was great. Taught me to how to fish, how to hunt. He wanted to make this place work so badly. He wasn't the easiest guy to get along with, he had an opinion about everything, but he was good to my mom and loved her unconditionally. I never heard them argue."

Summer gives me a genuine smile. "He sounds like a great guy."

"Yeah," I say, rubbing one hand over the stubble on my jaw as nerves suddenly slam into me. "I still can't believe you came all the way out here just to get me to talk."

Summer combs her fingers through the ends of her long ponytail, which hangs over one shoulder. "I didn't have a choice. I know I told your mom that I started my own company, but the truth is, it's barely off the ground. The opportunity to work with someone of your caliber, a client in the NHL . . . it would mean everything to me and really kickstart my career."

I think there's a compliment in there somewhere, but I'm still leery. "So, you said you know Les?"

She nods. "Yes, he's been like a mentor to me, and he just wants the best for me."

"He's a cool guy."

"He's the best. I actually had Thanksgiving dinner with him and his wife last year instead of spending it alone."

I take a step toward the door because I really do need to get back to helping Austen. But then I pause, glancing back at her. "So . . . if I did work with you, what would it involve?"

Summer's full lips lift. "Well, we'd talk. Have some counseling sessions. Probably like an hour each. Minimum of, I don't know, six sessions? And we could do them over the phone or Skype. I mean, I'm not staying. I only came to win you over with my shining personality and dedication to get the job. I wanted to show you I was serious about this." She grins, planting her hands on her curvy hips.

I'm distracted for a second, because she really is gorgeous. Fit, but with curves in all the right places.

I nod. "Okay, we can try. But the truth is, I don't know if it will help."

She reaches out as if to touch my shoulder, then thinks better of it and drops her hand. "If it's okay with you, and of course your family, maybe I can stay a couple more days and we can have our first counseling session either today or tomorrow face-to-face. You're helping your brothers today, right?"

"Yeah, but it won't take all day. We're planning on having a bonfire after dinner. You can come, if you want."

"That sounds nice."

"Well, I'd better get back out there. I'm helping Austen with his truck."

"You know how to fix trucks?" Her mouth lifts on one side with the question.

"Not at all," I say with a chuckle. "But neither does Austen. He's just too cheap to take it to a repair shop. We figure between the two of us, we'll figure it out."

Summer shakes her head with another smile. "Well, good luck with that. I look forward to tonight and our chat."

I give her a short nod. "Right. Catch ya later."

I leave as quickly as I can, and I don't look back. I can't let her get under my skin.

What do I care if Summer wants to stay for another couple of days? It's only a matter of time before she gets bored of watching my brothers and me haul wood, and fix broken-down tractors, and discuss sales strategies for the brewery. Maybe her boredom will make her run right back to the city where she belongs.

Far, far away from Lost Haven, and far away from me.

8

SUMMER

"How many times do I have to tell you? It was an accident."

Logan leans over the kitchen table, eyeing Graham, his jaw ticking with anger.

The tension at the dinner table has been on growing steadily since I arrived, the strain more and more obvious with every passing bite. But now, with nothing but potato skins and chicken bones left on our plates, the passive aggression has boiled over into good old-fashioned aggression. Most of it, to no one's surprise, is coming from a certain hot-headed hockey player.

Unlike his youngest brother, Graham keeps his anger more contained. "Some accident." He scoffs without so much as looking up from his plate. "Thanks to you, we're now set back months on that batch of ale. Do you have a damn clue how much time and money I've spent getting it just right?"

"I'll make up the difference," Logan growls through gritted teeth. "You know I'm good for it."

I don't need a deep understanding of the fermenting process to understand the crux of it. Something was knocked over, all their progress has been lost, and Logan is to blame.

"We don't need your money," Graham says firmly.

It's this sort of cool, collected sternness that riles Logan up, I've noticed, and his reaction is explosive. He slams his fist on the table, causing me to jump in my seat.

"Just give me a number. I'll write a check for double that so you can buy yourself some more stable fermenter tanks, while you're at it. Elevate your shitty little operation."

"Are you dense? That shitty little operation is our meal ticket." Graham finally looks up from his plate, his eyes blazing with white-hot anger. "Maybe you'd know that if you actually made an effort and came home once in a while."

Logan collapses back into his seat, throwing his arms in the air before slapping his hands on the table. The sound is loud enough to make me sit up a bit straighter. "Well, I'm home now, aren't I?"

Jillian reaches over to squeeze Logan's hand, her eyes pleading for peace between her sons. "And we're so glad you're here, honey."

Graham is less hospitable. "Sure. Some visit. Treating your family home as a rehab for angry assholes. Right down to the live-in shrink you've brought with you."

My heart plummets to my stomach, and I wish I could slip away or suddenly turn invisible. The need to get out of here hits me.

Before I can make an escape plan, Austen catches my eye from across the table, instantly sensing my discomfort and need to escape. He mouths the words "come on" and rises to his feet, tipping his chin toward the back door, and I follow without saying a word or looking back toward the kitchen. Exactly where we're going doesn't matter. I'll take any excuse to get out of the line of fire.

"Sorry you had to hear all that fighting and cussing," Austen says as we step away from the house.

"I work with athletes for a living," I remind him, zipping my jacket up to my neck. "Being around fighting and cussing is sort of the norm for me."

With a low chuckle, he motions for me to follow him. "I promise this is pretty standard when Logan's home. We have some strong personalities in the family, and when you add stress to that, it's a recipe for disaster. In this case, an argument. Don't sweat it, though. We'll leave them to argue, and we'll get the bonfire going."

It takes me twice as long as Austen to make the short trip from the house to the firepit—partially because his stride is twice as long as mine, and partially because I'm moving at a snail's pace so I don't slip on the icy path and end up with a concussion. The temperature plummeted after a wintry mix this morning, leaving frozen patches of snow here and there.

Austen chuckles when I finally catch up with him. "We oughta get you some new boots with better grip. That is, if you're sticking around."

Unsure of how to respond, I focus on the firepit, then the neat stack of wood a few yards away. "How can I help?"

He waves off my offer. "I've got it. You just grab a seat and try to stay warm till I get this thing roaring."

I do as I'm told, settling on the edge of one of

the worn wooden benches.

Austen gets all the wood he needs in one trip and goes to work arranging the firewood how he wants it. He's quiet as he works, and I figure now is as good a time as any to do a little more client research. I got a taste of the Tate family history from Logan last night, but now I want to hear Austen's thoughts.

"So, how did you guys end up all the way out here?"

Not as tactful of a question as I might ask one of my clients, but Austen isn't a client. He's my client's brother. And something tells me he might be an easier nut to crack than Logan.

"Dad bought the land about ten years ago. He had big plans for this place. Not just for the property, but for Lost Haven too."

"What do you mean?"

"His idea was to turn our property into some kind of tourist destination, a wilderness getaway of sorts. There's plenty around here, but this stretch of land . . ."

He trails off, his attention firmly fixed on building a teepee of logs. Once he's got the structure sturdy, he pushes up, wiping his palms on the worn denim of his jeans.

Urging him to continue, I say, "This stretch of land . . ."

"It just never got developed, I guess. So Dad took out a loan, bought up all this acreage, and we got to work building the house. The barn came next, then the garden. It was another two years before we cleared the land to get the guest cabins done."

I nod along, adding up the years in my head. "Sounds like a lot of man hours."

"Woman hours too," he says, correcting me. "Mom pulled her weight. We were just finally getting to a place to scale up this operation, start turning a profit. And then, well . . ." He pauses, swallowing a lump of emotion in his throat. "Well, then Dad passed. Now it's all up to Graham. A whole lot of pressure is on him. On all of us."

I pause for a moment, searching for the right words. But if there's one thing I know about losing someone you love, it's that the right words don't exist. There's just no way to make it better. Time and being gentle with yourself are really the only things that can help. It's a reality I know all too well. Yesterday, when Logan learned about my mom, I saw the hard look on his face falter, but just for a second.

"Sounds like big shoes for Graham to fill," I finally manage to say.

"Sure is," Austen says with a grunt. "And with all that change, money has been tight."

"I know Logan signed a nice contract."

"Sure, but he doesn't have most of that money yet. Besides, Graham's too stubborn to let his baby brother sink any money into this place, no matter how much we could use it."

Reaching into his pocket, Austen fishes out a box of matches, then crouches down again. Two or three strikes later, there's a spark, and then it catches on to the drier bits of wood. Soon, the tiny glowing embers grow into a low, steady fire.

By the time he shoves back to his feet, I've finally worked up the courage to ask the same question I'm sure he's asked himself a hundred times.

"So, what are you going to do?"

"Our damnedest," he says with a shrug, settling back onto the bench across from mine. "That's why we started the whole craft-beer operation. We're hoping that's the ticket, the secret ingredient that will make this whole thing profitable."

"Which is why Graham is so angry about Logan's mistake."

Austen smirks. "Now you're getting it."

The creak of a door interrupts our conversation, followed by the crunch of icy snow beneath furious footsteps. It's Logan, stalking toward us wearing a mask of fury. It's not till he gets closer that I realize his lip is split, and he's sporting the early signs of a bruise forming on his right cheek.

I have to bite my tongue hard to keep from gasping. I remember what Austen said about arguments being normal when Logan is home, but it's hard to believe violence is normal too. My stomach clenches into a painful knot.

"I think it's pretty obvious I won't be joining you tonight," Logan says gruffly, dragging the back of his hand along his lower lip. "Just thought I'd let you know."

With that, he turns and stomps back toward the house, and I'm right behind him. But once again, these darn boots betray me and slow me down. Logan is already halfway up the stairs by the time I step inside.

Most of the family has scattered, but Jillian is slouched over in the armchair, quiet sobs shaking her petite frame. After all the kindness she's shown me today, it takes every bit of willpower not to hug her. As a human being, I want to. But as a professional, I can't.

Instead, I just ask softly, "Are you okay?"

She looks up at me, her blue eyes red and brimming with tears. "Graham and Logan . . ." She bites her lip, choking back a sob. "Just a little fight, sweetie. Everyone's okay. But Logan is going to stay in the cabin next to yours for the next few nights. The boys just need some space."

Jillian is giving her son more grace than he deserves, but I can read between the lines. The look in her eyes says it all. Logan's anger is out of control, and it's not safe for him to be in the house anymore because he's like a grenade without its pin, ready to go off at any time.

Logan appears moments later at the foot of the stairs, shouldering a duffel bag. The anger has mostly left his face, leaving a mix of sadness and uncertainty. He gives his mom a quick kiss on the cheek, then turns back toward me. "Are you going to your cabin or staying for the bonfire?"

"I should head back to my cabin," I say, feeling a little weird about hanging out with his family if he's not there.

He nods once. "I'll walk you back."

We trudge through the woods side by side without exchanging a word. So much for us talking to-night. Instead of answers, I have even more questions.

First and foremost, how am I supposed to help a man who clearly doesn't want to be helped? He's not just angry—he's also violent. And not only with strangers, but with his own brothers, and I'm not sure I'm equipped to handle that. Which means ultimately, I'm going to let Les down, and even worse, myself.

"This is your stop." Logan halts in front of my cabin but refuses to look me in the eye. That would make him human, and that's something he doesn't want to give me.

Being practically ignored by him makes me feel helpless and unprepared. I wait for him to say anything more, but he doesn't. So I say good night and slip into my cabin, which is just as cold as it is outside.

Sure enough, my fire has gone out. Just another failure to add to my collection today.

A sigh of defeat pushes past my lips as I collapse onto the edge of the bed, burying my wind-chapped face in my hands. Every fiber of my being wants to break down, but I'm not risking freezing to death tonight without a fire. I start with the kindling as Logan told me, but after fifteen minutes, my hands are numb, and I still have no fire. With no other choice, I pull my phone from my pocket and call the main house.

Thankfully, Jillian picks up on the second ring.

"Everything okay, sweetheart? Need something?"

Her kindness makes my heart squeeze. Even with the night she's had, this woman stands ready to lend a helping hand.

I explain to her that the fire's gone out and it seems a lot colder tonight than last night. "Would you mind sending one of your sons down to help me?" I pause, then add, "Maybe not Logan."

"Of course, dear," she says, assuring me with her honey-sweet voice. "Sit tight, and I'll have one of the boys there shortly."

9

LOGAN

"Hey, Mom," I say when I pick up my cell phone.

I almost didn't answer because I figured she's going to complain about me fighting with Graham, although I'd probably deserve it. I shouldn't have lost my temper with him.

"Summer's fire's gone out," she says instead. "Be a dear and go next door and get it started for her."

I shift on the couch, straightening. "Why can't Austen? Or Graham? Or Matt?"

Mom lets out a long sigh. "You know why. Now go."

I groan. "Fine."

There's something about being around Summer that makes me feel on edge. And I know actually sitting down and talking to her in a counseling session would make me feel way too exposed. Even the whole honesty thing feels like too much. Sure, she's a beautiful girl—gorgeous, in fact—and I'd be lying if I said I wasn't attracted to her.

What would she possibly understand about my life?

But it's not fair to even think that. She's dealt with just as much, if not more heartbreak than I have. She has no one, and the thought of a pretty, delicate girl like Summer with no one looking out for her makes my chest throb. No one to help her if her car got a flat tire, or with the task of starting a fire. No one to be there for her, or celebrate holidays with...

Fuck, that's brutal. I shouldn't have rushed through showing her this morning. I should have had *her* do it with my help, instead of just doing it for her. I'm still being an asshole, and there's no way I can relax with the thought of her sleeping in her coat again. Especially with the temps dropping even lower tonight.

I grab my jacket and shove my feet into my boots without bothering to tie them, then I head outside, making the short walk next door. At the side of the cabin, I grab an armful of wood and then tap on her door with my boot.

She answers with a look of surprise. "Oh, it's you."

My left brow rises. "Were you expecting someone else?"

She blushes, shaking her head. "No, I just asked your mom if I could get a hand with the woodstove. I figured you didn't want to see me right now, and that she'd send one of the other guys."

"It's not that." I gesture inside since I'm standing here letting all the cold air in. "I'll help get it started."

She steps aside, and I head in. Summer closes and latches the door behind me while I stack the wood in a neat pile.

"Can I make you a mug of tea?" she asks.

I shake my head. "Come here. Let me show you how to get it started for next time."

She crouches down beside me, and I motion for her to follow my instructions.

"Add the kindling first. And then light it . . ."

She does, following each step until we have a nice fire going.

"Thanks, Logan." She beams at me with a grateful smile. "So . . . did you want to stay for a bit?"

I give her an apologetic look. "I'm sorry, but I'm not in the mood to sit around and talk about my feelings."

"Total honesty," she says. "You don't want me here, do you?"

I hang my head for a moment and then meet her eyes. "I didn't ask for this, Summer. Any of it."

She nods, and then quietly says, "You can't rejoin the team until a counselor clears you to get back on the ice. You might not have asked for it, but it's the only way for you to go back."

"Maybe I don't want to go back," I say without thinking. Just hearing myself admit that sends a cold chill down my spine.

She looks confused. "I thought you loved hockey?"

"I do. But maybe my family needs me more right now. I don't know. Maybe I need to be here instead of on the ice in Boston."

"Okay. I won't pry, but I'm happy to listen whenever you need to get things off your chest or out of your head. How about I make you a cup of tea, and I can look at your lip for you?"

"You don't have to do that."

She nudges me toward the couch. "It's just one cup of tea. For your trouble of coming to get the fire going."

I release a slow exhale and take a seat on the sofa. "It was no trouble, but sure. Why not?"

Suddenly, I'm not in the mood to go sit alone and stew in my emotions. And Summer . . . well, she's a distraction. I haven't determined yet if she's the good kind of distraction or the bad kind, so I guess I'm willing to stick around until I have that figured out.

In the small kitchenette, she adds water to the kettle and heats it, setting out two mugs while she waits. I like watching her move about the small space, the way her delicate fingers unwrap the tea bags, and how the curve of her ass looks in her jeans . . .I can feel my pulse quicken.

Stop, Logan.

I clear my throat as Summer, oblivious to my wandering thoughts, carries over two mugs of tea, careful not to spill them.

"Thanks," I say, my voice hoarse.

"Anytime. Thanks for *that*." She sits down on the sofa next to me and gazes happily over at the woodstove.

I take a sip from the mug and grimace.

"Not good?" she says with a laugh.

I pat the side of my jacket and then pull out a flask out of my pocket. "I'm not much for tea. But this might do the trick."

I dump a generous amount of whiskey into my mug and then offer it to Summer.

"Sure." Grinning, she holds out her cup.

I pour a small measure into her tea and then recap the flask. We each take a sip, silence settling between us.

"Thanks for coming over and rescuing me. *Again*. Let me look at that lip for you . . ."

"Uh. Sure."

Summer turns and kneels, facing me on the small sofa, and brings her palm to my cheek. Her hand is warm and soft and a little forceful as she turns my face toward her. My pulse spikes, and there's an unwelcome twitch in my jeans.

She inspects my lip carefully, which is swollen but not otherwise cut. "Are you going to tell me what this was about?"

This was me running my mouth at Graham more than anything, and Graham does *not* like to be questioned. Lesson learned. But I don't tell her any of that.

"Are you ever going to stop trying to be my therapist?"

"Point taken. How about we just work on being friends?" she says, dropping her hand from my cheek.

Missing the warmth of her palm more than I expected to, I say softly, "I might be able to do that."

She's still facing me, and my gaze drops to her lips. I want to kiss her. And for a second, I'm certain Summer wants that too.

But then she smiles, settling in beside me again before she takes a sip of tea. "Drink your whiskey."

When she nods at my cup, I down its contents in one long gulp, hoping it will drown out this bolt of misplaced lust that I'm feeling. Then I set my empty cup down and rise to my feet.

"I'd better go. Add another log or two to the fire before you go to bed, and it should keep the heat overnight."

Summer nods. "Thanks again."

"Good night," I say, heading for the door.

Usually, being home clears my head. Not this time, though. The fresh mountain air has been doing nothing but making me all hot and bothered. Actually, that distinction belongs to a certain five-and-a-half-foot curvy brunette who's invaded my family's property.

I add a log to my own woodstove and shuck off my hoodie and jeans before climbing into bed. For a moment, I consider jerking off, thinking maybe that will clear my head, but I'm not even in the mood.

I should be thinking about my team. Saint. Alex. Reeves. Even Lucian.

The guys need me. Or at least, it's a nice thing I tell myself.

Frankly, I'm starting to think my brothers might need me here even more. If only I didn't have a million-dollar paycheck on the line, and if my parents hadn't paid for every hockey camp, lesson, and league . . . I wouldn't feel so conflicted about walking away from that dream and giving it all up to stay here.

Almost as if on cue, my phone buzzes. I pull it

out and check the screen. It's my teammate Saint. Speak of the devil…

> **Saint:** Hey man. You good? We all miss you.

I chuckle and shake my head.

Really dude? **I reply.**

> **Saint:** Sorry. Reeves paid me to say that.

I doubt that, but I don't argue with him. Reeves is our team's captain and the dude is grumpy as hell most of the time. I highly doubt he's missing me.

> **Saint:** So, what's up, man?

I sigh and roll onto my side as I type out a reply.

Just hanging with the family. Helped my brother fix his truck today.

> **Saint:** Cool. Well, hope to see you soon.

Even if it was a brief conversation, part of me is happy that Saint reached out. It's nice to feel a connection with my team still. I feel so far away being out here in the mountains. I shove the pillow under my head and gaze up at the ceiling.

I'm still figuring things out after my dad's death—we all are. But I'm beginning to realize that Graham has it the worst of all of us. Taking over the family business is a big responsibility, and his life will never be the same. Not that the guy was a barrel of fun before Dad's heart attack, but now? Shit, I've been home for three days, and I've yet to see him smile or laugh.

And I shouldn't have lost my temper on him earlier. He didn't deserve that. He has a lot riding on him, and not in the fun, sexy way. I'm sure he hasn't been on a date in months. Not that this town has much in the way of single women.

Except Summer. She's single and smoking hot, none of which is all that helpful. Having her here is a distraction.

Though if I'm being truly honest, it's a good distraction, and part of me is grateful for her presence. Something to distract me from family-related stress. Maybe I should be embarrassed that she's here to witness it all, but I don't. She said she's not staying, so I guess it won't matter anyway.

I've wanted Summer gone from the moment I first saw her, so why does the idea of her leaving now make my chest feel tight?

10

SUMMER

The mountain air must be getting to my head.

That's the only logical explanation for what happened last night. Or rather, what I think almost happened.

Last night, when my hand was pressed against Logan's cheek, his soft blue eyes dropped to my lips, and I felt something transfer between us. A spark, big and hot like the glowing embers of my fire this morning. I swear that in that second, he wanted to kiss me.

What's crazier? The fact that I wanted to kiss him too. More than anything. I wanted to feel his firm mouth moving on mine, I wondered what it would be like to be the object of his attention... those big, rough hands, his muscular body...

As I brush the tangles out of my bed head and prepare to face the day, I replay that moment over and over in my memory.

There was something in his eyes, this brief flicker of . . . what? Interest? Desire? Whatever it was, it only lasted a fraction of a second, and the next thing I knew, it was gone, that stern mask firmly in place again as he turned to head back to his own cabin.

Part of me was disappointed over him leaving, but logically, I knew he had to go. Logan Tate is my client, and kissing him would be almost the least professional thing I could do. A slipup like that would ruin my career before it even began.

So, why am I still daydreaming about it a full ten hours later?

I sigh, tucking my hairbrush back into my toiletry bag, and check the time on my phone. I hardly get a signal out here, meaning the latest and greatest smartphone I invested in is practically a glorified pocket watch now. It's nine thirty, which I decide is late enough for me to venture to the house without worrying about walking in on breakfast.

Not that I'm not welcome at the breakfast table, but considering how the last Tate family meal went, I'm more than slightly nervous to face everyone again. Pair that with these weird feelings I'm having about a man who should be just a client, and I'm tempted to hole up in the cabin all day and hide from the Tate clan.

But I can't be a coward forever, so after a mini pep talk in the mirror, I shrug on my jacket and brave the icy path back to the house.

"Morning, Summer Sausage!"

Jillian is up to her elbows in dishes, but she greets me with the kind of sweet smile that says *we won't be discussing last night*. I'm relieved, to say the least, although a little perplexed about this new nickname.

I quirk a brow at her, slipping off my jacket and boots at the door. "Summer Sausage?"

"I'm trying to find a nickname that suits you," she says. "Not sure I've landed on the right one yet."

"I told her that not everyone needs a nickname," Grandpa Al mutters from his usual spot in the recliner.

Apart from the two of them, the house is quiet, and the table is cleared except for a sliced bagel and a bowl of fruit that my growling stomach hopes are for me.

"Can you do me a quick favor, Summertime?" Jillian tips her chin toward a jar on the counter containing a gooey white concoction. "Feed that sourdough starter a cup of flour from the tin above the oven, would you, hon?"

"I can do that."

I have to stand on tiptoe to reach the flour tin, but I complete the chore without too much trouble. As I work, Grandpa Al explains this sourdough starter's long history with the Tate family.

"The kids always wanted a pet," he says, a sweet look of nostalgia overtaking his face. "So their dad got 'em that starter from the bakery in town. Said if they remembered to keep it fed with flour, they could prove themselves responsible enough to graduate up to a goldfish."

"And guess who ended up feeding it the flour." Jillian rolls her eyes, suppressing a laugh, and Grandpa Al agrees with a snort.

"Yup. Hence, no goldfish and no other pets."

The story leaves a warm, pleasant feeling in my chest.

It's good to know there was a time when this house wasn't so stressful, when conversations revolved around potential pets instead of shoring up the family finances. I'm tempted to push the topic further, to ask Jillian what Logan was like back in those days, but before I can work up the courage, she steers the conversation elsewhere.

"Speaking of town, have you been in yet? That bakery has scones that would put mine to shame."

I shake my head. "I don't believe that for a second. But actually, a trip to the store might be necessary. There's a few toiletries I left behind, and if I'm going to be staying . . ."

"You can stay as long as you want," Jillian reminds me, her tone as serious as her eyes. "And as long as it takes to get our Logan right as rain."

An uneasy feeling turns over in my stomach. *Right as rain* is an awfully big goal for Logan, especially considering what went down last night, but I offer Jillian a reassuring smile anyway. I'm already nervous about letting Les down. Now I guess I have to add my client's mother to that list.

"There's a little general store about half an hour from here that should have everything you need." Jillian wipes her soapy hands on her cotton apron, gnawing her lip as she thinks. "We can lend you a car."

"Take my truck," Grandpa Al says, shooting Jillian a glare that could curdle milk. "Apparently,

I'm not allowed to drive it anymore," he adds under his breath.

"That's because we love you and don't want you dead in a ditch, you cranky old coot," Jillian fires back, then turns to me with a renewed sweetness in her voice. "Why don't you use the truck while you're here? Lord knows you don't need to be stuck here twenty-four seven." She pulls a set of keys from the hook by the door and places them in my palm. "You'd best eat that bagel before you go, though. We can't have you driving on an empty stomach."

A grateful smile breaks out over my face. Can't argue with that.

And gosh, it's been so long since I've been mothered by anyone, a small part of me is appreciative of the fact that someone, anyone, is fussing over me.

Once I've finished my breakfast and made sure there are no more chores Jillian needs help with, I slip out the door. In the gravel driveway, I unlock the truck and climb into the driver's seat.

Based on the dust gathered on the dashboard, I'm guessing it's been months since anyone has touched this thing, but when I slip the key into the ignition, it turns over easily. I adjust my seat and the mirrors, and even manage to find a radio station that isn't half bad. But when I reach over to throw this rust bucket in reverse, my whole body freezes, and not from the cold.

Nobody told me the truck was a stick shift.

I suck in a steadying breath. *Okay. Plenty of people drive a stick shift, right? I can probably figure this out on my own.*

I reach for my phone, ready to type **HOW TO DRIVE A STICK SHIFT FOR DUMMIES** into the search bar, but I'm quickly reminded of the lack of service out here. Either I can go find help or try to navigate this thing on my own.

Opting for the second option, I grab the gearshift and put it into first gear, then second. Suddenly, the truck stalls with a lurch, having moved only a few feet down the drive.

Great.

"What's going on here?" a low, cranky voice growls, barely audible over the clicking and sputtering of the truck.

It's Graham, looking even more displeased than usual as he frowns at me, his arms folded over his chest. I turn the old manual crank to roll down the window so I can explain my plight, stuttering as much as the engine.

"I—I'm just trying to get to town, and your mom told me I could borrow Grandpa Al's truck. And it's, it's . . ." I sigh, releasing the steering wheel in surrender. "Do you know how to drive a stick shift?"

"Yes."

Relief floods my system. "Thank God. Any pointers?"

His frown deepens. "Sorry, I don't have time for this."

Perfect. I've got the best, most sympathetic teacher ever.

Graham shakes his head, scratching at the stubble on his face. "I've got to start the fermentation process over. Sorry."

With that, he turns and heads toward the barn, and I'm right back where I started. Hopeless.

My stomach churns, my eyes stinging with the threat of tears. What am I even doing here? I can't start a fire, I can't drive a stick shift, and apparently, I can't be one-on-one with my client without wanting to kiss him.

Maybe I'd be better off calling a cab to take me

back to the airport. Except I don't even have cell service to look up the number of a cab company.

Freaking great.

Defeated, I leap from the truck and slam the door closed, giving the front tire a frustrated kick.

I'm not going to cry, damn it. Not now. Not over this. I've faced down much worse and come out all right.

"Are you okay?"

I turn on the heels of my boots, bracing myself to deal with grumpy Graham again. Instead, I find myself looking into the same soft blue eyes that nearly hypnotized me last night.

"Morning, Logan," I manage to say, trying not to notice how well he's filling out that flannel jacket. "Just, uh, trying to make a trip to town. Your mom didn't mention that the truck is a manual."

"Ah." He gazes at me thoughtfully.

It's quiet between us for a second, and I wonder if he's feeling as weird about last night as I am. Or maybe I'm just reading into signs that aren't even there. I push at the gravel at my feet with the side of my boot, trying to fill the silence with some kind of sound. But then he clears his throat, pulling my attention back to him.

"I could teach you, if you want. Or I could just give you a ride to town."

"I think I'm a little too frustrated to make a very good student right now."

His laugh is a low rumble in his chest that's sexier than I'd like to admit. "Understood. Let me tell Austen I'm taking off for a while. Be right back."

As he runs off into the house, I climb into the passenger seat, already feeling a sense of relief.

Moments later, Logan is sitting behind the wheel, working the gear shift like it's second nature. To my surprise, he leaves the radio station where I had it, playing old-school country songs. I thought he might be more of an angsty grunge type of guy, but I guess I still have a lot to learn about Logan Tate.

We spend the drive mostly in silence, apart from Logan occasionally pointing out an old mining town or a particularly famous canyon on our route. For someone who hasn't lived here for years, he sure does know a lot about this place. And it's a gorgeous drive so I'm easily entertained. Towering pine trees and rivers carved into canyons. I've never seen such beauty.

By the time we pull into the parking lot of a

small general store, I'm almost wishing the drive were longer. I like having Logan as my tour guide, and I'm already weirdly excited for the drive back.

Inside, we each grab a shopping basket, and I make my way through the aisles, grabbing all the things I forgot to pack. Heavier wool socks, some feminine products, and a bag of watermelon-flavored gummies to snack on in the car.

Logan follows close behind me, grabbing a bottle of mouthwash and a six-pack of beer, two things that directly cancel each other out, in my opinion. When we pass a rack of leather boots, he slows to a halt, running his fingers along the shearling fleece lining.

"What's your size?"

"Seven and a half, why?"

He scans the labels, then pulls out a box, tucking it beneath his arm. "Because I'm buying you these."

My mouth forms a tight frown. "You don't have to do that."

"Yes, I do." He glances pointedly at my high-heeled black leather ankle boots, which are sporting a few more scuffs than they had when my plane first touched down. "Total honesty? Your boots suck. You're going to trip and fall if you're still wearing those when the snow really starts. You need these."

"Then I'll buy them myself."

"No way. You wouldn't be here if it weren't for me. This is the least I can do after you came all this way to help me."

A hollow feeling forms in my chest as my gaze drops to the black-and-white tile floor. "I feel like helping you is the last thing I've done."

Although I'm avoiding his gaze, I can hear the confusion in Logan's voice. "What are you talking about?"

A frustrated sigh pushes past my lips. "First, I can't light my own fire. Then I can't drive the truck. Then Graham uses me as a talking point in your argument last night . . ."

"That argument had nothing to do with you," Logan says quickly, his voice stern and steady. "Graham was just trying to get under my skin."

"The point is, all I'm doing is causing you one headache after another. I'm supposed to be the one helping you, but you've just had to rescue me again and again. What's the point in even staying?"

Not a moment later, the slightest bit of pressure brings my chin upward. Here, in the middle of this general store, Logan is cupping my chin in his palm, tracing my cheek with his calloused thumb.

And there it is again. That spark. The same one that leaped between us last night. But this time, it's a little stronger, and not so quick to fade away. It lights a tiny fire in the center of my belly.

"You are helping me, okay?" His tone is softer and sweeter than I've ever heard before, so much so that I might actually believe him. "In more ways than you know. Stay a few more days. Please."

I swallow the emotion building in my throat. "Are we going to talk?"

He nods. "Tonight."

"Promise?"

"On one condition."

My lips purse as I hold back a breath. "That is?"

"You let me buy you these boots."

Done and done.

I knew when I was in over my head.

11

LOGAN

After dinner, Summer and I sit outside on the porch swing. She's all bundled up beside me, looking cute as hell in the new boots I bought her today, swinging her feet as we rock back and forth.

I'm not quite sure what I was thinking when I suggested she stay. Summer's presence here seems to trigger some overprotective part of me, something that makes me want to keep her close and make sure she's safe. If I send her back to the city, I can't effectively do that.

Maybe that's all it is. Just a friend looking out for a friend. No reason to read more into it.

Night has fallen, turning the sky a deep grayish blue. As it darkens, about a million little stars become visible. Glancing at Summer, I ask, "Are you warm enough?"

She nods beside me. "Thanks to you."

"It was nothing. I was happy to make sure you had what you needed from town."

I want to ask her if this means she's staying a little longer, but, well, basically I'm chickenshit.

We had something of a counseling session on the way back from town. At least, I'm guessing that's what it was. Summer asked me a bunch of questions about hockey and my life in Boston, and I answered them the best I could. It was surprisingly more comfortable than I imagined it would be, opening up to her like that. The whole honesty thing seems to be working. Plus she admitted to me that she's afraid of clowns and Mexican food is her favorite.

". . . and the town was adorable. That little house converted to a library . . ."

Startled, I realize she's still talking. "Uh, yeah."

Summer bumps her knee into mine. "And I appreciated our chat on the ride back too."

"For sure. I asked you to stay, right? I figure friendly chats are part of the gig."

At this, she gives me an uncertain look. "Logan,

as much as I *do* want to be your friend, you know I also have a responsibility to the team, right?"

"Um, yes?"

Her expression softens. "I'll have to give them a progress report on how I think you're doing."

I shrug. "That's cool. I get it."

"But it also makes you leery to share much with me, I suppose?"

I cross one ankle over my knee. "Believe me, if I have to talk to someone, I'd rather it be you than some therapist inside a stuffy high-rise office in Boston."

"I'd rather it be me too." She grins.

"So, just curious . . . how am I doing?"

My mom chooses this moment to interrupt us, and she's carrying two steaming mugs of tea.

"Do you guys want something to relax you?" she asks, holding out the mugs.

"No, we're goo—"

Summer interrupts me by reaching for a mug. "Sure. Thanks, Jillian."

I take the other mug and give my mom a look

that I hope communicates my desire for her to leave. Wearing a smug smile, she gets the hint and disappears back inside.

Summer takes a sip, and I touch her forearm. She peers at me over the rim.

"My mom grows this tea in her garden. There's probably CBD in it, just to warn you."

Mom has been known to shove a cup of tea at Graham or Austen from time to time, saying something like, *Here, darling. Drink this. You need to chill the heck out.*

Summer shrugs. "They put that in everything nowadays. Body lotion. Dog treats. I've never had it, but I've heard it relaxes you."

I nod and give the tea a suspicious sniff. I've never liked tea, and I don't have my flask on me.

Summer takes another sip of hers. "So, let's chat some more. We were on a roll."

"Sure. Fire away."

She's quiet while she thinks for a moment.

In the truck on the way back from town, she asked about my dad's death a little. But then she told me since she wasn't a grief counselor, that wasn't what we were going to discuss. She could relate to me on a personal level as someone who had also lost a parent, but the team had hired her to get me back out on the ice in tip-top shape. I appreciated how up front she was about everything.

Summer wraps her hands around the warmth of her mug. "Let's see. First, I think we should talk about how you handle it when things are outside of your control. There's an awful lot you *don't* control, and so things are going to go haywire sometimes."

I grunt in acknowledgment.

"So, that means you have to plan for adversity."

"I guess so," I say with a shrug. "Expect shit to go wrong and you won't be disappointed. That kind of thing?"

"Exactly. And in a game, you can't place too high of expectations on yourself. Let mistakes go quickly. I've noticed that athletes who are too hard on themselves can lose focus when things go wrong."

She's right. A couple of small mistakes on the ice, and I lose my composure. And once I lose it, I end up getting pissed off and find myself in fights on the ice.

Summer sets her empty mug on the table beside us. "Tell me what you're thinking."

"I agree with you. I know I need to let things go."

She nods. "It's more than letting go . . . it's *expecting* bad shit to happen. Knowing it's going to happen makes it less scary when it actually does, and you're somewhat prepared for it and know how to react."

"Makes sense. I think I can work on that." Apparently, I also appreciate a therapist who curses and talks so casually with me.

She touches my knee and squeezes, then giggles. "Jeez, you really are like a rock."

Her hand moves up my thigh, and since I'm ticklish, I squirm away on the seat.

When I meet her eyes, I realize they're glazed over, and she's smiling and giggling a lot more than normal.

"Do you feel okay?" she asks, wide eyed. "Because I feel amazing right now."

A sense of sinking dread settles into the pit of my stomach.

"Come inside for a second. We should warm up." I take her hand and help her off the porch swing, guiding her by the shoulders into the house.

It's quiet tonight. Just Grandpa and Mom. I leave Summer in the living room, where she admires a crocheted wall hanging, and head to the kitchen.

Frowning, I stop in front of Mom. "What the hell do you think you're doing?"

"Nothing, dear." Her voice is filled with surprise.

"Don't mess with this. Summer and I . . ."

"What did you do, Jillian?" Grandpa asks.

Mom's mouth lifts in an uncertain smile. "Nothing you wouldn't have done."

"Mother, the truth."

"Something that needed to happen. Everyone in this house is wound too tightly."

"You can't give people edibles without their consent," I growl at her.

"Special tea?" Grandpa asks.

"It's all natural. The elderberry and CBD from my garden."

Austen warned me once that Mom's version of CBD is basically just cannabis. *Fuck!*

"This is not good. If word gets back to the league that you drugged Summer, who is my psychologist . . . *Fuck*." I push my hands through my hair and begin to pace the kitchen.

Summer steps into the kitchen, looking first at Mom, then at me. "Your mom gave me an edible?"

Grandpa huffs. "I told you not to meddle, Jillian."

"I'm not." Mom raises her hands innocently. "And it's nothing. Just something to relax you. I'm so sorry, dear. It's got a very mild calming effect. That's all."

Summer leans one hand against the wall. "I'd better get home. I'm feeling a little strange."

"I'll walk you," I say, approaching Summer cautiously.

She pats my chest with one hand. "Thanks, Lo-Lo."

Lo-Lo?

I give my Mom a hard look. "We'd better go."

Mom touches her neck. "It's fine. I'm sure everything will be fine." She leans closer to me and whispers, "Keep me posted."

Summer leans on me as we walk, pointing out

the brightest stars, a spooky shadow, and a pine tree that she insists looks like an upside-down orca.

Shit, this is not good.

Once we reach her cabin, I add wood to the fire, and Summer immediately starts shedding her clothes. First the boots, then her jacket, then her sweater, all of which she leaves in a pile on the floor.

My heart hammers erratically as I follow her through the room, collecting the stray articles of clothing.

"Is it hot in here?"

"No," I say quickly, tugging her tank top back into place but not before catching a glimpse of a black bra that makes my pulse rate spike. "Summer. Stop. You need to keep your clothes on. It's cold tonight."

She smiles at me and touches her index finger to my nose. "Oh, Logan. Stop worrying so much."

I capture her wrist in my hand. "Summer." I give her a firm look. "Keep your clothes on, okay?"

When she nods, I release her wrist, but my reprieve doesn't last long. Humming to herself, she begins rubbing her hands over my chest. A bolt of pleasure zaps through me because it's been a long time since someone's touched me like this.

"You feel so good. So hard all over. Can I just pet you?" she says, and this makes her laugh.

Hell, even I chuckle. "I'm not a dog."

"You'd be a really cute dog." She grins. "Like one of those fluffy designer breeds, maybe?"

"Come sit down." I tug her toward the couch.

But once there, I realize my mistake. Summer is like an octopus, all hands. She climbs into my lap, straddling me, and her hands roam, petting my chest and pushing into my hair. Then she begins kissing my neck.

Fuck, that feels good.

"Summer, you need to stop." I grip her shoulders and meet her eyes.

But then she leans forward and captures my mouth in a hot kiss, and I'm powerless to do anything but give in and kiss her back. Her eager tongue touches mine, and I get hot all over.

I stand, lifting Summer with me, and set her on her feet. Stopping this is the only choice. No matter how good kissing her feels, I know it can't happen like this.

"We can't. Okay?" My tone is stern.

I expect her to nod in agreement or tell me she understands. Instead, she pushes her right hand inside the waistband of my jeans and slides it down into my briefs.

Jesus.

"Um, your hand is definitely in my pants."

"Mm-hmm," she purrs.

"And now you're touching my dick."

"*Oh.* It feels nice."

"Yeah," I choke out.

She moans. "Big. Hard. Stiff . . ."

Wrapping my hand around her wrist, I tug her hand free from my pants. "That's enough, Summer. You can't. *We* can't."

No matter how much I might want to.

Looking up at me through her lashes, Summer pouts. "Not even just this once? I mean, you're all alone out here, and I'm all alone. We're both single. And you're sexy as hell . . ."

"You think I'm sexy?" I lift one eyebrow. Her honesty is arousing.

"Uh, *yeah*. From the first time I saw you when

I watched one of your clips, then it was confirmed when I got here. Tall. Muscular. Cute face. You even have all your teeth, and for a hockey player, that's impressive."

I bite back a smile, but Summer's not done yet.

"Your family are all attractive too . . . good stock. But not your grandpa. I mean, for an older man, he's not *unattractive* or anything, but . . ."

I chuckle, stopping her with a hand on her cheek. I think she's trying to tell me she thinks my brothers and I are attractive, but I think I'll save her the embarrassment. "Summer."

"I'm babbling, aren't I?"

"Just a little." I smile. "You'll feel normal in an hour or two. And I don't want you to do anything you'd regret, okay?"

She nods once, meeting my eyes.

"Let me tuck you into bed."

Thankfully, Summer doesn't fight me on this. But she does shimmy out of her jeans and into a pair of flannel pants right in the center of the room, so I turn and give her some privacy. Once she's climbed in under the blankets, I tuck them in around her.

"Are you sure you're okay?" I ask, gazing down at her.

She nods, already looking drowsy.

"Text me if you need me."

"Like for sex?" she says around a yawn.

"Anything but that." The words are physically painful leaving my mouth.

She rolls her eyes. "Party pooper."

I chuckle and tell her good night. And then I head next door to my own cabin.

I'm still so aroused from our brief make-out session that my dick feels ready to explode, so when I settle into bed, I don't even bother to pretend I have self-control. If I don't jerk off, I'll never get to sleep tonight.

My right hand drifts south and pushes beneath the elastic of my boxer briefs. I'm still as hard as steel. A few quick strokes, and I'm imagining how Summer would have looked in that bra . . . How Summer's curves would have felt in my hands . . .

Pleasure rips through me as I let go, my hips lifting as I fuck my fist. She's gorgeous and kind, and she wants to help me. Apparently, it's a lethal combination, because a few more strokes and I'm already close.

If I were in the market for a woman, she'd be exactly what I'd want. Which is too bad, because she probably won't speak to me after she wakes up tomorrow and remembers all that happened tonight. But there's no room for reality inside my fantasy.

And in that fantasy, it's not my hand moving over my stiff cock, but Summer's hot mouth. A sharp throb of lust punches through me at the thought. It can never *really* happen, but *man*, is it a nice thought.

My brain plays out the fantasy in excruciating detail.

Would she be tender and soft and let me set the pace, or would she be eager and demanding, asking for me with her eyes and her words? Would she groan and beg for me? *I'm right here*, I would whisper, letting her take me in hand and guide me between her legs.

But I'll never know, which is for the best. It would only complicate things for me. And I would never use Summer to blow off some steam. She's a special girl. Definitely not someone I should sleep with once to satisfy some base-level craving.

No matter how badly I might want to.

How's that for total honesty?

12

SUMMER

It's late morning, and I'm working on my laptop at the cabin's small kitchen table.

The internet signal is surprisingly strong
today, which isn't the norm here in the middle of
nowhere. I'm thankful I have some work to keep
me busy this morning, because I may or may not
be hiding out today.

Okay, I'm definitely hiding. But who wouldn't
after last night?

I avoided breakfast this morning and got by
with tea and a granola bar because I wasn't ready
to face Logan just yet. Instead, I busied myself with
emails and an overdue phone call to Les, though he
didn't seem all that surprised to hear I'm still in
Colorado.

Jillian must have read my absence the wrong way, because she stopped by after breakfast was over with a thermos of hot coffee, already loaded with cream and sugar just the way I like. I guess it was her version of a peace offering. But I accepted her apology and the coffee. I know she meant me no harm. Her tea made me frisky, but that wasn't technically *her* fault. I'm embarrassed and honestly, well, *horrified* that I came on to Logan.

I've just gotten sucked into my social media feed when there's another knock at the door. I'm not sure if it's Jillian again, or maybe Logan, and my stomach twists itself into a knot.

I'm not quite sure I'm ready to face Logan after last night. But it's obvious I'm here, because where else could I have gone? So I heft myself up and trudge to the door.

When I pull it open, Austen is standing outside, not at all who I was expecting. He's every bit as tall as Logan, but a bit leaner and with more dark stubble along his sculpted jawline.

"Hey, um, what's up?" I ask, leaning against the doorway.

He frowns down at me. "I heard about the incident last night . . ."

The incident? Is that what we're calling my

molestation of his younger brother?

Oh God. This is worse than I thought.

"The, um, incident?" I stammer.

"Yes. My mom. The *tea*."

"Oh!" My face turns bright red. "*That*. Yes. You heard about that?" I squint at him, curious about what else he might have heard.

"Yeah, and for the record, I don't condone what she did. I just wanted to say I'm sorry. She means well, but she just . . . doesn't really have any boundaries."

I wave him off. "I'm fine. I promise."

"Well, that's good. I also wanted to let you know that Logan is going to be gone today. He's visiting our younger cousin who's away at Providence College, which is about two hours away."

"Oh. Okay. Thanks for letting me know." My relief is instant, but it's followed by a weird nagging feeling that I'm the one who drove Logan away with my inappropriate behavior. "Anything else?"

"Yes. I'm supposed to tell you that you're invited to Sunday dinner tonight. That is, as long as you're still speaking to my mom after what happened."

"I promise it's okay. Your mom apologized to me, just so you know. It's not a big deal. I know she meant no harm. And I asked if she'd give me some of that tea for when I go back to the city," I say with a wink.

Austen chuckles at this. "Okay. Cool. Well, I guess I'll see you tonight."

"Six o'clock?"

He nods. "Yep. See you then."

After I close the door, I lean against it. *Sunday dinner?*

A couple of thoughts hit me at once. First, who is this family? And second, why am I still here?

I didn't expect to be here more than a day or two—just long enough to show Logan I was serious and convince him to agree to work with me. And I guess I've done that? But it's been on his term, and now I have no idea where we stand. I've probably made things terribly awkward.

One last dinner with the Tate family, and I should probably leave tomorrow. Although going back to my life in Boston is about as appealing as eating dirty socks for dinner. But I have little choice, because as pretty and serene as it is here, I can't hide from my life forever.

Even if Mama Jillian's cooking will be sorely missed.

• • •

When I let myself into the house a few minutes before six, Logan is sitting near the fireplace with Austen and Matt, talking in low voices. Just the sight of Logan with his hair messy from his knit cap causes my stomach to twist. He's so ruggedly handsome—which is apparently a lethal combination for my libido.

I slip off my boots and bypass the brothers quickly en route to the kitchen.

The serenity of Jillian's kitchen is hard to explain. It's like an alternate universe where strangers are suddenly friends and friends are like family. I can't say I hate it. It's nice to feel welcome somewhere, even if this is only temporary.

She hands me a mixing bowl containing clarified butter and a small silicone basting brush. "Brush the garlic knots with melted butter, would you?"

I'm almost relieved when she puts me to work, which she inevitably does, like I'm part of the family and not an uninvited guest.

"Absolutely."

I accept the supplies and brush the top of each golden garlic knot with a generous amount of butter. The kitchen smells amazing, and Jillian hums to herself as she slices a ham. It's cozy and inviting, and I begin to relax the slightest bit.

I'm going to keep a low profile, eat a home-cooked meal that I've been invited to (it would be rude not to), apologize to Logan, and figure out what in the world to do next.

Easy peasy. Right?

So, why exactly is my stomach still twisted into an intricate knot?

• • •

"Can we, um, talk?" Logan stammers when he finds me still hiding in the kitchen twenty minutes later, where I've just removed the garlic knots from the hot oven.

"Sure thing," I say with a grin.

I smile when I'm nervous. It's one of those weird traits I must have inherited from my father, because Mom never did it. I set the oven mitts on the counter, but Jillian interrupts us by handing Logan a platter of sliced ham.

"Can it wait?" she asks. "Dinner's ready."

He gives his mom an uncertain look, but accepts the platter. "Sure."

She nods. "Better to eat while it's hot. My cooking's not *that* good."

But she's wrong. Her cooking is incredible.

Logan dutifully carries the platter of sliced ham to the dining room, following Jillian, who's balancing a basket with the garlic knots and a large bowl of smashed red potatoes in her arms. Everything is placed onto the table as the family finds their way into the dining room.

I know it's cowardly, but I wait for Logan to choose a seat, and then I make sure I'm not sitting by him. Instead, I take the empty chair next to Grandpa Al. After I help myself to potatoes and green beans from Jillian's garden, and some of that yummy ham, I listen attentively to all of Al's stories, which isn't too difficult because Grandpa Al is a hoot.

I can feel Logan's gaze on me during dinner, but I don't dare glance his way. I wonder if he's remembering my assault last night…

"And then in seventy-four, I met Lou, the cantankerous old fart," Al says, chuckling to himself and spearing another slice of ham with his fork. "Helped him fix up that Mustang."

After we eat, I volunteer to stay to help wash the dishes, hoping Logan will be gone by then. But he comes and finds me in the kitchen with my hands submerged in soapy dishwater.

"This isn't your job," he says with a scowl, and before I can say anything, he orders Matt to come into the kitchen and take over for me. Matt nudges me aside and takes my spot at the sink without any protest, so I dry my hands on a cloth dish towel printed with cheery pineapples.

If only my mood were as bright and cheery right now. My stomach is still in a knot, and I've barely kept my hands from shaking.

"Come on. I'll walk you to your cabin," Logan says, his voice low.

I guess we're going to have that chat now. My stomach gives a painful little twist.

I thank Jillian for dinner, and squeeze Grandpa Al's wrinkled hand before following Logan to the door.

Logan walks me back to my cabin, then gets the fire roaring again. We both take off our coats and boots. Since he doesn't seem to be in a hurry to leave, and there's that familiar scowl back on his handsome face, I make myself busy.

"I'll get us some wine," I call over my shoulder on my way to the kitchenette. I'd picked up a bottle of wine when we were in town, seems like a might fine time to open it.

When I return with two glasses of red wine, Logan is standing in the center of the living room, looking uncomfortable.

"Let's sit," I say. As awkward as this is, I know the only thing to do is to launch into a rambling apology, so that's exactly what I do. "Listen, I'm just going to say some things. First, I'm truly sorry about last night."

Logan's eyes widen as he watches me.

"I was totally out of line, and I'm so—"

His large, calloused hand on my wrist stops me.

"Summer." His voice is deep, low and raspy. "You have nothing to be sorry for."

"I came on to you, and—"

He shakes his head. "Believe me, I'm not upset

about that. I'm more upset about my mom giving you her special tea."

A crease forms between his brows, and I realize he's telling the truth. He's not mad at me.

A tidal wave of understanding washes over me. Here I spent the past twenty-four hours growing an ulcer and planning my escape, only to find out Logan doesn't hate me. My relief is instantaneous.

"Oh, thank goodness, because I was terrified at how I behaved and I know it was unprofessional, and . . ."

I'm still rambling when Logan touches my cheek and turns my face toward his.

"Summer," he says softly.

My name on his lips is the most distracting sound, all rough and yet sweet like sandpaper and honey. It sends a tingle rushing through me.

"You had a strange reaction. That's all it was. Breathe, okay?"

Suddenly mute, I nod. I grip the stem of my wineglass so hard, I'm surprised it doesn't shatter.

That's it? I was so scared to talk to him today, so his response is the last thing I expected.

"Are you sure?"

"I'm sure. Unless you want to talk about the fact you said you think I'm sexy." He waits for me to reply, a smirk tugging at his lips.

A blush warms my cheeks. I did say that. And I meant it too.

I draw a slow breath, because Logan's still waiting. Still trying to fight off a smirk. "Well, I suppose that doesn't matter. I mean, attraction aside, we're working together, right? Nothing can happen between—"

I don't get to finish the rest of that sentence because Logan's mouth is on mine, hot and insistent. Purely on instinct, I press closer, and when my lips part, he takes full advantage.

His tongue touches mine, and my knees go weak.

Secretly, I've wondered what it would be like to kiss Logan, and now I don't have to wonder any longer. The man is extremely skilled. One of his big hands weaves into the hair at the back of my neck, tilting my head just so, and I almost dissolve into a puddle on the floor. He tastes like red wine and man, a combination my poor little neglected heart can hardly handle.

I move closer, urgently needing to erase all the distance between us.

His tongue moves against mine in deep, drugging kisses that make my toes curl in my socks. He makes a low, breathless sound, and for one glorious moment, all the noise in my head quiets, and it's just me and him.

It feels so right to be here, doing this with him. But a second later, my brain switches back on and I pull away, putting an inch of space between us.

His forehead touches mine, and I let out a long, shaky exhale.

"We shouldn't be doing this," he whispers.

"I know. We can't."

I need to put an end to this before I do something foolish, like drag him to my bedroom.

Before I can process what's happening, Logan pulls us over to the couch, and then I'm sitting in his lap, happily grinding my hips against his.

The stubble on his face scratches pleasantly against my chin, the feeling both foreign and erotic. It's been a very long time since I was with a man, but Logan doesn't seem to notice or care about my lack of finesse. His hands roam from my shoulders down to my waist. I can feel a hard ridge beneath me—the press of his erection against me—and I groan into his kiss.

"We can't do this," I say slowly, groaning out the words.

"No, definitely not," he says in a strained voice.

So, why aren't either of us stopping?

He pulls off my shirt and drops it to the floor, then places a soft kiss to the top of my collarbone and another on my shoulder. His mouth is warm and soft, and I'm flooded with endorphins.

While every part of me wants to continue this—preferably pants-less and inside the bedroom—a small, stubborn part of my brain clicks on and reminds me that we *can't* do this. It would be wildly unprofessional of me to give in to my desires.

I really hate being so dedicated sometimes.

"We can't," I murmur, pressing one palm to the rough stubble on his cheek. "I'm here to help you get back to work playing hockey." I pause, drawing a breath. *Not to ride you like a prize stallion at the rodeo.* "I'm sorry."

His gaze tracks from my lips up to my eyes, and even though I'm sitting in his lap shirtless and still panting, he nods his understanding. "I get it. And I'm sorry too."

I retrieve my shirt from the floor at our feet and tug it back on. Maybe I should feel self-conscious, but I don't, not around Logan. While I straighten my shirt, he banks the fire, telling me it should last the night, and then tugs on his boots.

I meet him at the door, and the wistful look in his eyes is almost enough to make me forget my principles and tug him back over to the couch.

He tucks a loose strand of hair behind my ear and gives me a warm smile. "Good night, Summer."

"Night," I say, my voice sounding surprisingly steady considering the erratic pounding of my heart.

• • •

When I wake in the morning, I wait for a sense of regret to hit me, but it doesn't come.

Small mercies, I guess.

I dress in warm clothes and leave the cabin for the house, already dreaming of whatever pastry Jillian has decided to make this morning. But I stop short when I see all the firewood in neat stacks outside my door—a large pile of split logs and a huge basket of kindling. Logan's work, obviously.

How long does he think I'm staying? There's

enough wood here to last me all winter.

Or maybe he just really needed to work off some tension?

I hesitate, but decide to knock on his cabin door. A few footsteps approach from inside, and the door swings open.

"Summer," he says, sounding somewhat surprised.

"Hey. Good morning."

Maybe I should feel embarrassed or regretful about the kisses we shared last night, but even in the light of day, any negativity is just absent.

"Thank you for the firewood." I tip my chin toward the neat stacks.

"Sure. Wanted to make sure you'd be warm. The weather is turning." He glances at the sky before meeting my gaze again.

"I'm going up to the house. Can I bring you some coffee?"

"I'm good."

I shift my weight, nerves suddenly setting in. "Are we okay? Last night . . ."

He stops me. "We're fine. Last night was my

fault. It won't happen again," he says, his voice sure and steady. "In fact, let's meet tomorrow for another counseling session."

"Sure," I say. "What time?"

He scratches his chin. "How about tomorrow afternoon? I'm helping Graham today, and then I'm going hunting with Matt tomorrow early in the morning. I'll be back by lunch, though."

Filled with a renewed sense of purpose, I nod. "Okay, I'll see you then."

13

LOGAN

It's still dark out the next morning when my brother Matt wakes me with three quick knocks on the cabin's front door followed by one slow one. Our secret knock as kids.

My eyes are closed, but I smile before grunting and rolling over. It's too damn early for this, but I agreed to go hunting with him today. He said we had to get an early start, but if I'd known he meant before dawn, I might have reconsidered.

The door opens, and he calls out, "Wakey, wakey." His voice sounds way too cheery for whatever ungodly time this is.

"Go away." I tug the blankets over my head, as if that will block out his enthusiasm.

"I brought coffee."

"Leave it on the table and then go away," I say with a groan.

A low chuckle is followed by the sound of his boots crossing the floor. "Come on, it'll be fun. And I need your help."

"You do not," I grumble.

Matt hunts without me all the time. Turkeys in the spring, elk in the early fall, and then deer later on.

He chuckles. "Come on. Get up."

Realizing he's not going to stop until I do, I shove off the blanket and sit up. "Fine, but give me that coffee."

Fifteen minutes later, I'm dressed in warm clothes and hiking through the woods beside Matt. Thankfully, the thermos of coffee he had for me is strong, and it's working to improve my mood.

"So, did you and Graham make up, or what?" he asks, referring to our fight the other night. One that I'm not proud of, for the record.

"Yeah, we did. All good now." I spent the day yesterday helping him brew beer.

He shoots me a curious look. "Do I want to know what you were fighting about?"

"Nope."

The less stress for this family right now, the better, I figure.

"All right, let's talk about Summer."

Uncertainty squirms inside me. Last night, things went too far. I'd hoped kissing her would take the edge off the need that had been clawing at me for days. But it didn't, not at all. It only made that need grow more insistent, fiercer. Darker somehow.

"What about her?"

Matt smirks. "First, she's smoking hot."

"Don't." Stepping over a fallen log, I give him a warning glare.

"What? I have eyeballs."

"Well, keep your *balls* to yourself."

He chuckles. "Oh man, don't tempt me. Do you know how fucking horny I've been?"

"No, and I don't want to know."

But the truth is, I do know, because I'm in the same boat. Or at least a similar canoe. An adjacent watercraft.

Fuck. I'm being weird. Pay attention to what he's saying, Logan.

Matt takes a swig of coffee and carries on, completely unaware of the entire monologue that just took place inside my brain. "You don't live here, so you don't understand how there's like one woman for every ten dudes out here."

I roll my eyes. "This isn't like Alaska in the Gold Rush, bro. What about dating apps?"

He laughs. "Yeah, I tried that, dumbass. Believe me, it's bad. The single men in this town far outnumber the eligible women. Half the town has blue balls."

Not the conversation I expected to be having this morning. "That sucks," is all I manage to say.

"It does. Not all of us are pussy-slaying NHL stars."

"Well, I'm not anymore. That second thing, anyway. I'm suspended, remember? And that first one . . . believe me, I'm not slaying anything."

"No puck-bunny action?" His tone is filled with surprise.

I shrug. "Not really. There was this one girl last year, but I got the sense she liked the idea of posting about me on Instagram more than she actually liked being with me."

"When's the last time you . . . *ya know*."

"This is a conversation you and I will never have," I mutter.

He gives me a pointed look.

"*Fine*."

I realize I'm being evasive. Matt and I have always been honest with each other. Back when he was eighteen and freaked out that he'd gotten Tessa Elford pregnant, it was *me* he came to for advice.

Thankfully, she wasn't pregnant, but I listened to his worries and gave him advice during the stressful week when she thought she was. Maybe talking this stuff out is part of being a good brother. Or maybe that's just Summer's advice getting into my head. Either way . . .

"It's been a while," I say begrudgingly.

"So, why don't you make a play for Summer?"

"No." My tone leaves little room for negotiation, but Matt is undeterred.

"Why not?"

"Because," I mutter rather brilliantly.

My brother rolls his eyes. "Okay, then let me ask her out. Like I said, she's gorgeous. *Someone* should go out with her."

"No."

He scoffs. "I don't have to ask your permission, you know. I could just ask her out."

The idea of that is *not* a pleasant one.

Summer isn't mine, and she's free to date whoever she wants. But the idea of her with another man? Well, I don't like it.

The surge of territorial instincts that hit me take me by surprise. Summer's a grown woman. She can choose who she dates. And it's not like that man is going to be me—for obvious reasons.

"And take her where, exactly?" I ask. After all, Matt is the one who just mentioned how very little this town has to offer.

"I don't know. Back to my bedroom? Bed of my truck?"

The thought of that makes my blood boil. "You're an asshole."

"I'm kidding. God, you should see your face right now. There are some cool places. The mineral hot springs is one. They don't have that in the city. Or the farmer's market. Duke's Tavern. Lots of places."

"Hmm." I make a noncommittal sound.

"Even a picnic, if it wasn't so cold out."

"Yeah, did Mother Nature just decide to skip fall this year or what?" It's so chilly out, we can see our breath.

Matt nods beside me. "Yeah, it looks like it."

We walk in silence for a few minutes longer. I can't decide if he's still thinking about Summer, or just opting to stay quiet because we're getting closer to the deer stand and he doesn't want to scare away the animals.

When we reach the spot where Matt's constructed a blind up in an old oak tree, he goes up first, and then I climb up after him. It's tight quarters—little more than just some elbow room between us as we huddle inside. The plywood sides don't offer anything in the way of warmth, and I find myself hoping that we can spot a deer and be out of here soon. A great woodsman, I am *not*.

Matt surprises me by striking up another conversation, this one about Graham's newest plans with the beer operation.

Jeez, Chatty Cathy over here.

I give him a stern look. "I know I haven't been hunting in six years, but aren't we supposed to keep quiet?"

Matt shrugs. "Hunting is more about the bonding time. And I haven't seen you in a while."

Feeling a little guilty, I nod. "I know. But Graham will be pissed if we come back without a deer."

He huffs out a breath. "True story. But Graham's pissed off about everything these days."

Matt's comments aren't directed at me. I know he doesn't mean to make me feel guilty about the fact I've stayed away, but I do. I haven't been here to help, and it's becoming increasingly obvious that the family has been under a lot of stress. I can't help but think about the fact that my family seems to need me more than my team does.

Since I left Boston, there's only been a few halfhearted texting attempts from the guys. Saint reached out the other day, and since I've heard from Alex and Reeves.

But while I do miss them, miss being out on the ice, I can't let myself think about hockey right now. I need to focus on getting a deer to feed my family this winter. Need to focus on being there for Matt. And Graham.

And I definitely can't let myself think about Summer, so I settle in beside my brother and watch the horizon where the sun is beginning to turn the sky orange as it rises to greet us.

14

SUMMER

How long does hunting usually take?

This is the question I've been asking myself for the past few hours. I've been holed up in my cabin since just after breakfast, preparing for my afternoon counseling session with my client. The only issue? My client is MIA. Logan said he would be back by lunch, but it's quickly approaching two o'clock, and I still haven't seen or heard from him. Needless to say, I'm all sorts of anxious about it.

Heaving out a sigh, I collapse onto my bed and wriggle my phone out of the front pocket of my jeans. It takes some creative positioning of my phone next to the window, but I manage to scrounge up just enough cell service to send him an "are you home yet?" text.

Ten minutes later, still no word, but there could be a multitude of reasons for that.

There probably isn't cell service out in the woods, or he may have turned his phone off altogether. Or maybe he left his phone in the cabin so it wasn't a distraction. All totally practical explanations. But that doesn't stop me from wondering if he's actually ignoring me because he's decided not to work with me anymore, all thanks to our little incident last night. That would be a death sentence for both of our careers.

Ugh. There's only one cure for this level of overthinking. I need to put on my big-girl pants and head over to his cabin.

Getting out of bed on three. One . . . two . . . two and a half . . .

With one final frustrated groan, I shove up from the mattress and pull on a fresh pair of wool socks. Then come my boots, coat, and the gray wool hat I found shoved in the back of the top dresser drawer. It smells slightly of mothballs, but the sky is extra overcast today, and the cold feels like it could freeze my ears off without it.

When I catch a glimpse of myself in the mirror, I'm startled by how well I could pass for a local in this outfit. A true Lost Haven resident. Lost Havener? Lost Havenite? Whatever you call them, I'm beginning to look like I fit in here, and it's somehow both comforting and concerning. If I'm not careful, I could get a little too comfortable here. Which is why I need to focus on why I'm in Colorado in the first place—to work with my client.

Tugging the scratchy wool hat down a little further over my ears, I trudge out the door and toward Logan's cabin. But it doesn't matter how hard I pound on the door, there's no response.

To my surprise, though, the doorknob twists easily, so I take a serious risk and let myself in, peering into what would be pure darkness if not for the dim light of the lamp on his nightstand. It casts a warm yellow glow over the deep gray comforter, where Logan is propped up against the pillows, sleeping soundly on top of the covers. It's as though he had sat down for just a moment and then nodded off.

"Logan?"

He doesn't stir at the sound of his name, so I try again a little louder. "Logan? Rise and shine."

He doesn't budge.

When I reach his bedside, I pause for a moment, admiring the way the lamplight casts shadows along the curve of his jaw. I've never seen him so at peace, all cozy and cute in a Burton Snowboards hoodie and gray sweat shorts.

As I watch his wide chest rise and fall with steady, sleepy breaths, warmth radiates from my chest to my fingertips. The Logan Tate I've gotten to know the past few days is sexy, without a doubt, but this is a different version of him. A soft, gentle, sleeping giant, he snores softly through his barely parted lips. He's downright adorable, from his messy bedhead to his long bare feet, dangling off the edge of the bed.

Snap out of it, Summer. I need to act fast before he wakes up and catches me staring.

"Logan." A firm shake of his shoulder does the trick, and his thick eyelashes twitch before his eyes fully open.

"Jesus," he grumbles, wiping one hand over his jaw. It's surprisingly cute. "What time is it?"

"Almost two."

"Shit." His face scrunches up as he rubs the sleep from his eyes. "We got back from hunting, and I was absolutely beat."

"Nothing to apologize for. I'm glad you got some rest. Are you still down for our session?"

"Of course."

"Then why don't you get ready and then come find me?"

He nods in agreement, and I head out the door, stepping back out into the chilly afternoon air.

Here's hoping the wind will blow the blush right off my cheeks.

I admit it—I'm more than a little smitten with Logan. The trick is going to be learning how to hide it.

Twenty minutes later, our roles are reversed, and Logan is the one letting himself into my cabin. He's layered up a bit more than I would have expected, though, and it's quickly obvious why.

"I was thinking we could go for a bit of a road trip instead of sticking around here."

I fold my arms tight over my chest. "I thought we were going to have a counseling session."

"We are. I just think we should have it off property."

"Neutral territory?"

He shakes his head. "Just someplace I thought you might like to see. Maybe even a bit of excitement."

I nod. "A change of scenery could be nice."

I have to bite my tongue to keep from arguing the point that Lost Haven has very quickly become one of the most exciting places I've ever been. Bonfires, stick shifts, and surprise CBD tea? It's a lot more excitement than I've experienced in a long time. Tack on the steamy forbidden make-out session we had last night, and I can confidently say that this tiny little mountain town easily beats out Boston in terms of excitement.

But I don't say any of that. Instead, I shrug and say, "I'm down for whatever."

"Cool." A sly grin tugs at his full mouth. "Follow me. You're driving."

Well. That's the worst news I've heard all day.

Reluctantly, I follow him out to the driveway, eyeing public enemy number one—that manual rust bucket of a truck.

"Can't you drive?" I plead, but Logan shakes his head.

"You can do this, I promise. I'm going to teach you."

When I slide into the driver's seat, baffled as ever by the numbers on the stick shift, my shotgun passenger wastes no time launching into his lesson.

"First, you've got to ground the clutch," he

says, as if that should mean something to me.

When I stare at him with wide, clueless eyes, he laughs and rephrases his instructions.

"Use your left foot to press all the way down on that pedal, and put the gear shift in neutral."

For as hotheaded as he is on the ice, Logan is a surprisingly patient teacher. I follow each and every one of his steps to a tee, stalling only a handful of times, and barely resist the urge to bang my head against the steering wheel until the car horn sounds.

Here I am, supposedly the calm, cool, and collected counselor, and Logan is the one guiding me along the learning curve.

It's hardly what I was expecting out of today, but by the time we hit the highway, I'm a few steps short of a master of the manual transmission. All it took was some encouraging words and a few gentle squeezes of my thigh from the handsomest driving teacher this side of the Rocky Mountains.

With all my intense focus on being in the right gear at the right time, I've hardly paid attention to where Logan's directions are actually taking us. When he has me pull over on the side of a wooded back road, I'm sure we must have taken a wrong turn somewhere.

"Where are we?"

"The hot springs," he says as casually as though we've just pulled up to a grocery store.

I squint out my window, looking for . . . well, I don't really know what I'm looking for. I've never been to a hot spring before, but from my understanding, they're usually surrounded by fancy hotels and spas. Outside my window, all I see is miles and miles of mountains and rocky paths through the woods.

"Don't hot springs usually have, like, resorts built around them?"

"Those are the hot springs that the tourists know about." He gives me a coy smile and a wink, then throws open the passenger door. "The best ones are kept a secret unless you're local."

My heart does a little kick in my chest. If I wasn't feeling like a Lost Havenite earlier, I sure am now.

I follow Logan along one of the rocky trails, ducking beneath branches and occasionally veering from the trail markers. He's right about one thing—this is definitely the kind of place that only a local would know about. No one from out of town would ever think to go off trail like this.

After a short but tiring hike, the thick rows of pine trees give way to a clearing of rocks and determined wildflowers peeking through the mud and snow. Right in the middle, the hot spring is clouded by its own steam, giving off an air of mystery.

"This is gorgeous," I whisper, taking in our surroundings.

I've never been anywhere even marginally similar to this. A faint smell of sulfur hangs in the air, and I realize it must be from the trace minerals. Even the rocks surrounding the water are slightly calcified.

"Are we getting in?" I ask.

"I sure am. You'll like it, come on."

Logan toes off his boots, then peels out of his jacket and sweatshirt until he's down to nothing but his faded gray boxers.

Try as I may to keep from staring, my gaze momentarily dips to his deliciously chiseled abs and the tempting bulge beneath his waistband. He may be a rookie, but this man has the body of an all-star. The show doesn't last long, though, because soon he's climbing over the rocks and sinking into the hot spring, shuddering at the drastic change in temperature.

"C'mon." He beckons me in with a coy smile. "The water's fine."

Yeah, and so is the man in it.

To my surprise, it feels almost too normal to be stripping down in front of him. I untie my boots, then hang my coat over a tree branch, followed by my sweater and my jeans. Thank God I didn't wear a thong today, or worse yet, granny panties. In a sensible black bra and matching cotton underwear, I can almost pretend I'm in a bikini.

As I'm sizing up the rocks around the hot spring, looking for the safest point of entry that will get me out of the cold the fastest, I can feel Logan's heated gaze on my body. It feels nice, almost safe, since none of his family is around to tease him for staring. When I catch his gaze lingering on my breasts, he looks down and coughs into his hand, acting innocent and distracted. I can't help but laugh. He's a much better hockey player than an actor.

I climb over the rocks, trying not to slip, and when I sink into the water next to him, I'm careful to leave more than an arm's distance between us. Because, you know. Reasons.

"So, I'm sure it's been a lot of stress to be back here," I say, sinking my toes into the clay at the base of the spring. "A lot of old emotions to face with your family."

His gaze narrows, one dark eyebrow arching. "Are you going therapy mode on me?"

"You did say that we could still have a counseling session," I remind him.

"Right, right." He stretches out his arms, settling back against the rocks.

I can't help but notice how his pecs flex, the rounded caps of his shoulders carved out by the shadows of the trees. It takes my full attention to keep my eyes locked on his instead of ogling his physique for this whole session.

"Things are . . . tough," he grumbles, scratching at the stubble along his jaw. "I don't even know anymore. Most of the time I feel like I'm just going through the motions with my dad gone."

"I get that. It's okay to miss him. It's okay to be angry. But it's not okay to give up on your dreams or stop living your life. Your father wouldn't want that for you."

"I know," he says softly.

Our conversation seems a little strange. It's like I've known Logan forever, and my advice is from one friend to another. As someone who cares deeply about him.

"It's just that being away from the family is hard. But being back here is hard too," he says.

"None of this is easy. It's not supposed to be," I say gently.

He nods, a lump of emotion bobbing in his throat as he forces a hard swallow. "I guess you're right. I just wish it could be simple." He's quiet for a moment, one damp hand working through his messy brown hair.

He looks so hopeless that, as unprofessional as it is, I find myself moving closer to him and bring my arms around him. Logan relaxes against me, releasing a deep sigh.

My brain starts spinning. Maybe because he's this big strong man, but it's never occurred to me that I would have to be careful with him. Yet it's obvious I do. I curl myself into his chest and wrap my arms around him and just hold him. Breathing in his winter-air scent, I murmur into his neck that everything will be okay.

I stroke my fingers through his hair and tell him he's incredible and that everyone is proud of him. He lets out a deep grateful exhale and holds me tighter. I tell him that he's so strong, and that it's okay to be vulnerable too, sometimes. He makes a low wordless sound.

I can actually feel him healing and being knitted back together right in front of me.

It's a side of Logan I didn't imagine I'd ever see, and I'm so grateful that he's comfortable enough around me to let his walls come crumbling down.

When we finally part a few minutes later, there's an easiness about him that wasn't there before.

"Thanks, Summer."

I meet his serious expression with one of my own. "You're welcome."

I can sense a change in him. Before me sits a man who, at one time, I thought was all hard edges. But I was wrong. There's a softness about him too.

He doesn't let many people see this side of him, which I can understand. The less people know about you, the less they can pry. It's a self-preservation technique. Keeping people at arm's length is one of Logan's coping mechanisms. But knowing I'm someone he's willing to let into his inner circle makes my heart squeeze a little. I feel warm all over, and it's not just because of the hot water we're lounging in.

Sometimes I wonder if I'm qualified for my new job. But when I'm talking to Logan, I feel qualified, helpful even. Maybe it's sporting of him to amuse me into thinking so, I'm not sure, but I definitely appreciate how useful he makes me feel.

When he finally breaks the silence, it's with a question I never could have seen coming. "How did you lose your mom?"

A burning sensation sizzles in my chest. I wasn't at all prepared to talk about this, but he's been so vulnerable with me, the least I can do is return the favor.

"Car accident," I choke out, examining my hands to avoid his gaze. "Drunk driver. She died on impact."

"I'm so sorry," he whispers. "How do you . . . how did you get through it?"

I meet his worried gaze and lift one shoulder. "I don't know. One day at a time."

"God, Summer. I'm sorry. That's awful."

"You can't appreciate the sweet if you never have the bitter."

He nods somberly. "You said she was your best friend?"

I lift my chin. "Yes. She was. And believe me, it's been tough, and the pain will always be there. But time helps, and so does knowing that she wouldn't want me to be sad about it all the time." I muster up the courage to meet his eyes, his gaze soft with compassion. "The important thing to remember is that you're not dealing with the hurt all alone. You have your mom and your brothers and your grandpa and—"

"And you," he interrupts.

My breath catches, and I realize this isn't just a counseling session anymore. It's so much more. This is two people connecting on the deepest level, despite the hurt from their pasts. This is real. Raw.

More than anything in the world, I desperately want to close the space between us and kiss him again, the way he kissed me last night. Hard and sure and with abandon.

But I know I can't. And that's a kind of hurt I don't know how to deal with.

"How did you know about this place?" I blurt out, looking for any way to change the subject.

Logan seems to understand and follows along without hesitation. "We've been coming here since before my dad bought the property. It's been a few years for me, though. I've sort of been avoiding it."

"Why would you avoid somewhere as beautiful as this?"

The smallest nervous chuckle rumbles in his chest. "You sure you want to know?"

I nod, eager to be let in on what feels like a big secret.

Logan clears his throat. "Well, uh, because Graham told us that he lost his virginity here. Kind of ruined it for me."

"Ew!" I squeal. "Don't ruin it for me too!"

"You asked," Logan says with a chuckle.

Soon, we're both laughing and splashing water at each other. I feel like a kid again, flirting with a boy I like at the neighborhood pool. Maybe I was wrong before about none of this being easy. Because this, right now, feels as simple as it gets.

As the sun sinks lower in the sky, we enjoy the relaxing mineral water together. Small talk comes easily, but comfortable silences fill the space between us too.

Finally, once we're thoroughly pruney, we slip back into our clothes and begin the hike back. By the time we reach the truck, the moon and stars are starting to peek through, and I gladly take Logan up on his offer to drive. I may have made serious progress on the whole driving a stick thing, but I'm not sure I'm ready to tackle it in the dark just yet. Plus, I could use a little time in the passenger seat to reflect on the conversation we just had.

A mile or two down the road, Logan takes a turn in the opposite direction of home. "Are you hungry? I thought we could swing by a taco stand on the way back."

"I never say no to tacos. It's a personal principle of mine."

He laughs, and I wonder if he suggested that because I told him Mexican food is my favorite.

"And I don't come to this side of the mountain without swinging by the Gonzalez family's taco stand. So it looks like our principles align." He grins, and I feel that dimpled smile way down in my belly.

A laugh bubbles out of me, the kind of true, honest laugh that only comes around once in a great while.

But it's immediately followed by a swift dose of reality. Because I just realized how much this whole day feels like a date, something I haven't had in forever. But I know it can't be, no matter what my heart wants.

Even if today was great, and his big family

is everything I've ever wanted, and Logan's blue eyes are completely dreamy, I know better than to let my silly fantasies turn into anything more than daydreams.

Maybe I should leave, fly out on the next plane and distance myself from the handsome Logan and all my confusing emotions. But walking away now is the last thing I'm prepared to do.

Somewhere along the way, Logan Tate and his family have taken up space in my heart. Impossibly and against all common sense, I'm feeling things for this man that I have no right to feel. Achingly hot when he levels me with those deep blue eyes. Haunted by all he's been through. Desperate for the feel of his mouth on mine.

And I'm feeling almost none of the things I should be feeling. Professional and detached, or even unbiased. This is more than problematic. I've staked almost my entire professional reputation on this assignment, and yet here I am—in totally over my head.

When we reach the cute roadside attraction, which is just an old silver Airstream that's been converted into a food truck, Logan orders for us while I take a seat at a nearby picnic table.

I pull a deep breath into my lungs and try to

quiet my brain, glancing around.

White Christmas lights twinkle in the darkness, strung from the Airstream to a couple of large pine trees. The entire setup is adorable. They certainly don't have quaint little places like this in the city. It feels like a well-kept secret—the kind of place where you have to know someone who knows someone.

Thankfully, I do.

Logan returns with a tray filled with warm flour tortillas and plastic containers with red and green salsa. He hands me a bottle of water and explains what he's ordered for us—tacos with brisket and pulled barbeque chicken, and carnitas tacos topped with queso fresco that smell so good, my stomach grumbles.

"Cheers." He hands me a water bottle, and then opens his, downing it in one long gulp. Grinning, he says, "Dig in."

And I do, trying to pretend that this doesn't feel like the best first date I've ever been on.

I've always thought when I fall in love there would be candlelight and wine and maybe fancy appetizers. Now I wonder if someone can fall in love with the scent of sulfur still on their skin at a roadside taco stand, eating from paper plates.

Because from where I sit . . . it sure seems like it.

15

LOGAN

"That's a nice one. Six points?" Austen asks.

"Eight," Matt says proudly. He adjusts the bill of his ball cap as Austen and Graham scope out the deer we got this morning.

Well, Matt got the deer. I spotted it first but nudged him in the elbow. He'd drifted off to sleep about two hours into our hunt—how, I'll never understand. The deer blind was cold, drafty, and uncomfortable.

I pointed to the grassy bluff out in the distance, wanting him to be the one to take the shot since he loves hunting. I don't really care for it, truth be told. And now, seeing how proud he is with Graham looking on, I know I made the right call in waking him.

"That should stock the freezer nicely. Well done, boys." Graham doesn't smile, but he does nod to indicate his approval. It's probably the most praise we'll get out of him.

Summer enters the barn, carrying a stack of books Mom loaned her after dinner. There's a title about the medicinal properties of different herbs, a slow-cooker cookbook, and Lord knows what else. I'm still not sure if Summer was only pretending to be interested or actually wanted to borrow all of these from Mom's personal library. She's got such a positive attitude all the time, it's hard to tell.

The moment Summer realizes what we're all standing around staring at, she stops suddenly and one hand flies to her mouth. The deer is hanging upside down from the rafters, so it's kinda hard to miss.

"Hey, sorry." I raise one hand toward her. "I should have warned you or something."

She swallows hard and shakes her head. "It's okay." Taking a cautious step closer, she gestures toward the animal. "Is this the deer you got?"

I nod. "Matt got him, but yeah."

"I'm both thoroughly grossed out and impressed."

Matt chuckles. "I'll take that as a compliment."

"As you should." She treats him to a wide grin, and I'm struck, not for the first time, how truly gorgeous she is.

When her eyes meet Matt's, his lips lift into a smirk. "Hope you like venison."

She scrunches her face. "I've never had it, but I'll try anything once." Her eyes narrow. "Wait, you cook it first, right?"

This draws a hearty laugh out of Graham. "Of course we cook it. We aren't Neanderthals."

"It tastes similar to steak. Maybe more gamey. But it's not bad," I say, since Summer's still wide-eyed.

She nods, but I notice she doesn't come any closer. Not that I blame her. It's a lot to see a large dead animal on display. Nothing at all like shopping for your meat at the grocery store.

Austen adjusts his ball cap and announces he's taking off.

"Where are you going?" Matt asks.

Austen tilts his head toward the house. "Mom made meatloaf. I haven't eaten yet."

Matt nods. "Enough said."

"Enjoy, brother," Graham calls to Austen's retreating form.

"I'm going to build a bonfire," I say, heading toward Summer. "Everyone's invited."

Summer turns to follow me. "Will we have marshmallows to roast?" she asks with a smile.

"For you? Anything. Let's see if we can scrounge some up."

While I get started on the fire, Summer insists on going up to the house to ask my mother for marshmallows. Matt drags over a couple of chairs.

When she returns with a big bag of fluffy marshmallows and a smile, I feel like I've taken a hit to the chest. She's just so damn pretty, and my thoughts turn indecent almost immediately. But then she settles in beside me and hands me a flask of whiskey my mother filled for her.

I accept it gratefully and take a big swig, hoping it will extinguish whatever the hell this weird feeling is inside my chest. Too bad it doesn't work.

Graham pours mugs of beer from a growler he's just bottled. "It's a day or two too early," he warns everyone, but we all assure him it's good, and it is. Nutty and vibrant with hints of grapefruit.

Summer rips into the bag of marshmallows and

places two on a skewer, then offers me the bag. I dig out a marshmallow and eat it whole.

"Hey, that's cheating. You have to roast them first," she says, scolding me playfully.

Grinning, I help myself to another, and Summer's laughter is the best sound. Light and slightly husky.

Those indecent thoughts are back—with a vengeance. This time, rather than another shot of whiskey, I shove another marshmallow into my mouth and chew. I expect to be hit with a sugary rush, but I'm so distracted by her, I swear I don't taste a single thing.

I try to focus on the conversation happening around me. The guys talk about hunting, and Graham chatters on about the beer-making process to anyone who will listen. Summer occasionally asks insightful questions. She has a knack for keeping the conversation going.

I can't help but notice the soft look in her eyes. She's happy here; I can see it. We all can. But does it mean anything? I'm awful at reading signals, apparently.

After she's roasted and eaten several marshmallows, she licks her sticky thumb and then rises to her feet, announcing that it's getting late.

"I'm going to head in. Good night, guys." Then she meets my eyes, and her voice softens. "Thank you for the fire. It was lovely."

Suddenly speechless, I simply nod.

We all watch as Summer wanders away in the direction of the cabins. I'd be lying if I said I didn't notice how well her backside fills out a pair of jeans.

Graham smacks the back of my head.

"What the hell was that for?" I rub at the tender spot.

"Walk the lady home, you idiot."

My brothers are all thinking the same thing, and I'm sure they're questioning my manners. Apparently, my interest in Summer beyond a professional capacity is the worst-kept secret ever. I toss the bag of marshmallows at Matt to a chorus of snickers, and head off after Summer.

It's not that the thought didn't occur to me. Of course it did. It's dark, and she's alone. But I'm feeling a whole lot of things I have no right to. I'm worried that if I go after her, I won't be able to keep my hands to myself. Nevertheless, my brother's are right. I should walk her home. I jog to catch up with her.

I surprise her near the chicken coop, and she lets out a startled gasp, her hand flying up to her heart.

"Sorry," I say in a soothing voice, placing my hands on her shoulders. "I didn't mean to frighten you."

"W-what are you doing?" Her pulse flutters wildly as she pauses beside the chicken coop, with its cheery robin's-egg blue paint that Mom is so proud of.

"It's dark. I should walk you back."

"Oh."

Summer's tone is filled with surprise, but when her gaze meets mine, I can tell she's not opposed to this idea. I catch a glimpse of appreciation in her eyes.

I feel like even more of a fool that I didn't immediately leave the fire and insist on joining her. But I'm here now. And Summer is looking so beautiful under the glow of the moonlight that I forget what I'm supposed to be doing for a second.

As if she has some sort of gravitational pull, I find it impossible to stop myself from kissing her. My palm touches her cheek to draw her close, and Summer comes willingly, moving toward me until we're chest to chest.

I slide my hand into her hair as her hot mouth meets mine enthusiastically. Her kisses are sweet, and hurried, and I drink them down.

Waves of lust pulse through me. The taste of sugar and female is a potent combination. And Summer isn't just any woman. She's kindhearted and funny, and she's put up with my family all week without complaint. I can't help my body's response to hers.

When her lips part, I deepen our kiss, my tongue meeting hers in eager strokes. Her hands curl into fists as she grips my shirt, hauling me closer.

I walk us back—three steps—until her back meets the wall of the chicken coop. I'm sure she can feel the situation below my belt, but Summer's only response is more kissing. It's a scenario I'm very much okay with.

Moonlight paints us in a hazy glow. While being pressed up against the side of a chicken coop is probably the least sexy thing ever, neither of us seem to care.

She makes a needy sound in the back of her throat, somewhere between a whine and pure want. It sparks something inside me, and I bring one hand under the edge of her sweatshirt, my knuckles tracing the soft skin of her stomach.

Breaking our connection, I press my forehead to hers. "You're dangerous."

"So are you."

I know what she means, this burning attraction that neither of us seem capable of resisting.

Being near her—there's something about it. Something risky. It's like my libido has magically rebooted. Not just rebooted, but roared to life with a hunger more potent than I've ever experienced before.

I press my mouth to hers again as my hand travels north. Palming the weight of her breast earns me another of those moans that I'm quickly growing fond of.

"Do you want me to stop?"

"No." Her voice is sure. Steady.

Her skin is so soft and warm, and I'm lost to her kisses. When my fingers skim down to the waistband of her leggings, she makes a breathless sound.

"Can I touch you?" I murmur with my mouth still on hers.

"Yes." Her voice is a whisper, but there's no

uncertainty in her tone.

With my pulse thundering, I press my hand lower, beneath the elastic of her leggings and panties. I bite back a groan when I feel how warm and wet she is.

It triggers something inside me.

As she grips my shirt to haul me closer, my fingers slide over silken flesh until Summer is trembling and gasping in my arms. I love touching her like this, making her feel good.

A few minutes later, the air around us shifts. She's close. I feel it the second she lets go and begins to come undone. Everything south of my navel twitches with satisfaction. It's beautiful watching her overcome with her release.

But I barely have time to savor it, because I hear the rustle of footsteps on fallen leaves. Summer's eyes snap open to meet mine.

"Hurry," is the only word I get out before I begin pulling her along the path back into the darkness toward the cabins.

When we reach mine, I twist the doorknob and she follows me inside—no invite necessary. It seems she's as eager to pick back up where we left off as I am.

We slip off our boots at the rug by the door, and I tip her chin up to meet my gaze. Her shaky smile grows, and then we're both laughing.

I rub a hand through my hair. "Sorry. I guess I got carried away back there . . ."

But I don't get to finish my apology because Summer's mouth is on mine.

I kiss her back like my life depends on it, and maybe it does, because I've never felt this good, this free with anyone else ever before.

Breaking away briefly, I ask, "Will you stay?"

She nods once in understanding. This moment is too real, too perfect to just brush aside.

My hand slides from her hair to the column of her graceful neck, then her shoulder, and I enjoy the feel of soft cotton beneath my fingertips. Summer wets her lower lip with the tip of her tongue. Her mouth is beautiful, and wicked thoughts dance through my head.

My hand slides lower until it comes to rest on her lower back. The movement thrusts her forward slightly, and her soft curves graze my chest, my abdomen, and lower—where surely she can feel how hard I am beneath my jeans. She responds with a tiny shiver.

I can't help it . . . all the crackling electricity between us has me eager and aching. Tugging her over to the couch, I sink onto it with her. The cabin is dim, lit only by the light above the kitchen sink, which casts broad shadows, and little flickers of glowing orange from the embers in the woodstove.

Summer settles into my lap. We grind together and kiss, both of us willing to pretend—at least for now—that this isn't a dangerous game.

When she brings her hand between us to rub at my swollen erection, I bite back a groan.

I open my mouth to say something. What, I'm not sure. But when she slides from my lap to the floor between my parted knees, I forget how to breathe, much less speak.

Who needs words right now, anyway? Certainly not me.

As Summer's slender fingers go to work unbuttoning my jeans, I help her, dragging my pants and boxers down until she finds what she's after. I'm so hard and swollen, and Summer moans as she wraps me tenderly in her hand. Then she pauses, the blunt head of me pressed right above her sweet mouth.

The sight makes me dizzy. For all my fantasies, I never imagined we'd actually be here, doing this. I want to slow time, to savor this. This beautiful girl, on her knees before me . . . her eyes mischievously drinking me in.

But then her tongue moves over me in one long, lazy stroke, and my eyes sink closed.

"Shit." I growl, pushing my hands into her hair as I let out a groan. "Yeah. That's perfect."

"You like it?" she asks, teasing me, her tongue flicking over me seductively.

"So much."

Her eyes meet mine briefly before sinking closed. I groan again, trying to keep my hips from thrusting up.

Seated on the couch, I'm able to watch how she takes me—alternating between deep sucks and slow gentle kisses that I feel all the way to my toes. She makes little sounds as if the act of pleasuring me pleases her somehow. It's sexy as hell. She's spoiled me of enjoying this with anyone else, ever again.

"Deeper," I say on a groan, and she obeys, sliding her lips all the way down my shaft. I curse again, my ab muscles contracting with how good it feels.

I have no idea what I did to deserve this, but with Summer's mouth working me closer and closer to the edge, I've never felt so good in my entire life.

She moves faster now, adding her fist, and I inch dangerously closer to the edge.

With the worst timing ever, my cell phone rings. I ignore it at first, and Summer does the same. My entire body is practically vibrating with pleasure. But the ringing doesn't stop, and I'm forced to wrangle the damn device from my jeans pocket.

"Yeah?" I bark out to whoever has the balls to interrupt such a perfect moment.

"Oh, good. I caught you."

It's my mother.

And Summer still has my cock in her mouth.

Fuck.

Fuck!

"I'm a little busy . . . did you need something?" I manage to say in a strained voice.

"I just wanted to talk about how I'd like the venison butchered. You're taking it to Cinnamon Creek, right?"

My brain spins and short-circuits. Cinnamon Creek is the meat-processing operation two towns over. It's a long drive, but they do the best job.

"Uh," is all I manage to say as Summer's mouth moves over me in hot, enthusiastic strokes.

With my fingers under her chin, I lift her head. There's a soft sucking noise as my cock slides from between her lips, and I groan at the loss of suction.

Belatedly, I realize that my mom is still talking. *Just kill me now.*

"And I'd really like tenderloin, chops, and a couple of roasts. I don't need much in the way of ground—"

"Mother." There's a desperate edge to my voice, and I clear my throat before continuing. "Can we talk about this later?"

There's a long pause on the line. "Oh. Is Summer there?"

"I'm hanging up now."

Mom makes a joy-filled sound at the idea of Summer and me coming together. "Okay, 'bye. Wear a condom, honey. I'm not ready to be a grandma just yet!"

"'Bye, Mom." I toss the phone down with disgust, and Summer's answering smile makes me chuckle. "I'm so sorry about that."

But Summer is already guiding my still rigid cock right back into her mouth.

Shit.

I fist her hair, desperate for her again.

You'd think this would be the most disturbing exchange ever, but I go right back to enjoying the most perfect blow job in the world, delivered by the most perfect girl in the world.

16

SUMMER

Did I plan on having an orgasm up against a chicken coop?

Well, no.

Logan's skillful fingers and his hot, eager mouth proved to be too much for me to handle. All sensibility flew out the window.

But do I regret it? Also, no.

Although deep down, I know I *should* regret it. And that's really bothering me. I'm not this person—the bold woman who flew across the country to track down a potential client. Or the one who's losing her sense of direction because her client is so stunningly attractive.

Last night was an eye-opener for me. One thing became abundantly clear.

I need to get out of here—hightail it back home before I do something incredibly stupid, like jeopardize my entire career for a little nookie. Even if said nookie would be really, *really* good.

"I think I'm going to head back to Boston."

This news announced at the breakfast table goes over like a lead balloon. Only Logan and Jillian are left, with Grandpa Al reading the newspaper in his recliner. Yes, I waited till most of the boys had cleared out before making my announcement, but only to try to avoid too much awkward conversation about it.

Unfortunately, it doesn't seem like my plan is working. While I pick at my currant muffin, I can feel the energy in the kitchen shift, and not for the better. When I look up, Jillian is staring at me like I just announced I was walking barefoot back to Massachusetts.

"You're leaving already? What on earth for?"

The list of reasons could stretch from here back to the East Coast.

For one, I'm developing some not-so-professional feelings toward my client, who is currently sitting across from me, taking long swigs of coffee and dodging my gaze. He's definitely been a bit off this morning since what happened between us last night.

Which brings me to reason number two—the fact that Jillian is ultra-aware of reason number one.

But I'm not going to mention either of those reasons right now. Instead, I'm sticking to the practical truth.

"Logan's cleared to conduct the rest of his sessions with me virtually, so there's no need for me to stick around and wear out my welcome."

"You're not wearing out anything," Jillian tells me, reaching over the table to give my hand a gentle squeeze. "We love having you around. Don't we, Logan?"

The sweet, slightly pushy smile that she gives her son is met with silence from him and a visible cringe from me.

I love Jillian, but I don't love the fact that she knows what's going on between Logan and me. We haven't gone five minutes this morning without her suggesting that Logan take me to see the local sites like the waterfalls in Aspen Park, or mentioning a new restaurant in town the two of us could check out.

And I'm guessing she may know exactly what

her phone call last night interrupted.

I should have gotten off my knees the second she called, and booked a flight instead of proceeding to . . . I'm not even going to think about that. What happened between Logan and me last night was so wildly unprofessional, even thinking about it feels dirty in a hundred ways, both good and bad. And the fact that I would gladly repeat my actions this evening means it's absolutely time to get out of Dodge.

A labored grunt comes from across the room as Grandpa Al pushes up from his recliner. I've hardly seen him leave that thing since I first arrived, aside from meals, and I'm actually a little surprised to see how agile he is. I could have been convinced he was confined to that old leather chair.

"I'm going to check on the chickens," he says firmly. "And Summer here is coming with me to the coop."

My stomach does a flip in my belly at the mention of the chicken coop. "I am?"

"Sure are." He points his thumb toward the door. "Get a move on. We've got eggs to collect."

"Since when do they produce eggs in the winter?" Logan asks, his voice suspicious.

"They can do anything if you keep 'em warm and happy." Grandpa Al pulls a scratchy-looking wool coat off the rack and shoves his arms into it. "Just like me. C'mon, Summer, let's go."

Not one to argue, I lace up my boots and follow him outside.

It's a short walk to the chicken coop, where Grandpa Al shows me how to shift the straw in the nest box to locate the eggs, then swap out the old straw for fresh bedding.

I'm all too happy that our conversation is strictly business. Any mention of Logan right now while at the scene of last night's crime would probably turn me redder than the currants in the muffin I had this morning.

Then out of nowhere, Grandpa Al asks a question I couldn't have seen coming. "You ever been hunting, Summer?"

Staring at one of the hens pecking at the feed in the corner of the coop, I bite my lower lip with worry. "We're not going to hunt these poor chickens, are we?"

He wheezes out a laugh. "Oh, heavens no. I'm talking about deer."

Whew. Thank God. I already have too many

feelings tied to this chicken coop. I don't need to throw *devastating sadness* into the mix.

"I grew up in the city. There's not really a lot of opportunities for hunting deer there."

Grandpa Al runs a hand over his beard. "Well, you'll have plenty of opportunities if you stick around here."

My chest tightens. What gave this family the idea that I would be a lasting fixture in Lost Haven?

"I'm not going to be sticking around," I remind him. "Like I was telling Jillian, I think I'll go back to—"

"Last year was an especially good deer season," he says, disregarding what I just said. "But there was this one time, I thought I'd lined up my shot just right."

He sets down the basket of eggs and mimics holding a rifle, his whole body jerking back as he lets the imaginary bullet fly.

"Boom. Should've been a clean shot. But he must've been a fast bugger, because I just got him in the leg. Injured the poor guy. I had to put the animal down. End his suffering."

"I don't think I need any more details," I say with a wince. I'm not a vegetarian, but much more of this kind of conversation may turn me into one.

"The point is, I set out to kill a deer that day, and I did. It didn't happen the way I planned when I first lined up that shot, but I got it done, and I got a good story out of it. Do you understand?" He offers me the slightest smile, but I'm totally lost.

"I can't say I do."

"Sometimes, you think you have a plan and everything goes sideways. But you can still do what you set out to do if you stick to your goal. And you might even get a good story or two out of it."

There's that flip-flopping feeling in my stomach again.

Does Grandpa Al know what happened last night too? Or maybe he just senses something is up between Logan and me. Either way, I wish I could click my heels together and magically transport out of this conversation.

"I don't think you should leave just yet," he says finally. "Give it a day to really decide. I don't think your work is finished here, even if it's not going according to plan."

I want to tell him that I didn't come out here with a plan. That my only plan was to get Logan to agree to meet with me, to get his anger issues under control and get him back on the ice.

But Grandpa Al is right about one thing. I think I have some unfinished business here in Lost Haven.

"Fine." I sigh, reaching down to grab the basket of eggs. "One more day. Just one." I hold up my pointer finger to further drive my point home. "Okay?"

Grandpa Al's satisfied smile is as wide as a country mile. "Deal."

Well, if I accomplish nothing else today, at least I made an old man smile.

We bring the eggs back to the house, where Logan has disappeared and Jillian has already moved on from breakfast and brought out her stand mixer to start baking bread.

"Want to lend me a hand, Summer? If you're not in too much of a rush to get to the airport, that is." She gives Grandpa Al a wink, and it's never been clearer that there's a full-family effort taking place to keep me here.

But for some reason, I don't mind. It feels good to be wanted, to be part of a family, even if it's not mine. I feel at home here. And that thought is as troubling as it is comforting.

"I've never made bread before," I say, swapping out my coat for an apron. "But I'm ready to learn, if you'll teach me."

"Oh, sugar." Jillian squeezes my arm, her rosy cheeks lifting as she smiles. "I'll teach you anything if it means keeping you around another day."

My heart gives a little squeeze at her kind words. To feel needed, wanted . . . well, it's a very powerful thing. Back in Boston, I'll be alone much of the time in my little apartment. And while that's never bothered me before, the idea of it now doesn't sit well.

While Grandpa Al settles back into his chair, Jillian flips on the radio. Before long, I'm up to my elbows in flour, learning to knead bread *the right way*, as Jillian keeps saying. I can't help but laugh at the idea that there's a wrong way to knead bread that would end with the oven exploding or something worse.

As we work, Jillian treats me to plenty of family gossip about her sons.

According to her, Austen hasn't been on a date since last year; meanwhile, Matt hasn't brought the same girl home twice since he moved back to Lost Haven. When she tells me about her secret tally of Matt's one-night stands that she keeps on the side of the fridge, I have to stop kneading dough just to laugh. And sure enough, there are a whole bunch of tick marks on a scrap of paper.

By the time the bread is in the oven and I'm ready to wash up, I'm wishing I promised Grandpa Al two days instead of just one to mull over my next move.

Yes, being here has brought many awkward moments, but it's also brought some of the sweetest memories I've made in forever. I've been so busy with work the past year that I can't remember when I last had this much time to just *be*. To bake, to laugh, to spend time around a bonfire, sipping whiskey and swapping stories. It's a life so unlike anything I've ever known, and it's given me nothing but a whirlwind of confusing emotions that I shouldn't be feeling.

"The oil leak in the mower's all fixed!" a familiar voice shouts from the door to the garage.

Moments later, Logan is standing in the kitchen, his jeans and hands smeared with sooty oil. When he spots me, there's a twinkle in his blue eyes that makes my heart pound a little faster.

"You're still here."

"Of course I'm still here. I wouldn't leave without saying good-bye."

The slightest hint of a smile twitches at the corner of his mouth. God, this man. He shouldn't make me feel this way, but he does.

"Glad to hear it, Summer."

The sound of my name on his lips sends heat climbing up my spine. It takes me right back to last night, the way he moaned my name while I . . .

My phone buzzes in my pocket, a welcome interruption to a very inappropriate train of thought. It's a text from Les, asking how things are going.

"Excuse me," I murmur, untying my apron before reaching for my coat. "I think I need to make a work call."

"Hurry back," Jillian says with a grin.

Smiling, I slip into my boots and head outside for a bit of privacy.

Les picks up on the second ring, his familiar gritty voice cutting right to the chase. "How's Colorado?" he says instead of hello. He's never been one to mince words.

I hesitate, but only for a second. I know I can be honest with Les.

"It's complicated," I say, pacing up and down the gravel path. "But I think I'm making slow progress with Logan."

"Slow?" he huffs out. "You've been there several days now, Summer. Are you telling me you still haven't convinced him to do counseling?"

"No. No." Frowning, I backtrack. "He's agreed to counseling. But the counseling itself is slow moving. I've definitely seen some of where his anger issues come from, but I don't think we've gotten to the heart of the—"

"Summer." Les interrupts, his voice stern. "I appreciate your dedication to your work, but if you've helped him at all, just sign off on the papers. It'll be okay. I know you did the best you could."

"W-what?" I stop dead in my tracks, surprised at what I'm hearing. "But we haven't worked through all his anger issues yet."

"You're not going to. That's the thing about Logan Tate. His issues go deeper than anything you're going to solve over his suspension. But if you've managed to get him on board with counseling, you've done more than any of our other counselors have done."

I can't help but feel a little proud of that. "Really?"

"Yes, really. And that was why you flew out,

right? To get him to agree to counseling? You've done that, so just sign the papers and you can head on back."

"I'm going to. I'm just working through some details first."

"What kind of details?"

I pause, then decide to play the patient confidentiality card. "We've encountered some bumps along the way," I say, which isn't entirely a lie.

I would say developing feelings for my client definitely counts as a bump. A large hill. Small mountain, maybe.

"Understood," Les says. "I'm glad to hear you're working so closely with the client."

A lump builds in my throat. If only he knew that *closely* is an understatement.

17

LOGAN

O ur musty old barn isn't so musty and old anymore.

Sure, there's still that same draft leaking through the crack between the oversized sliding doors, and yes, the air still smells like fermenting beer mixed with stale chicken feed. But Graham's hours of work on this place have done a serious one-eighty on the smelly old barn where we used to play hide-and-seek. With a smattering of freshly painted picnic tables and those trendy twinkle lights hanging from the rafters, this could easily be rural Colorado's trendiest brewery, right in our backyard.

"Graham, you're an absolute genius." Summer gapes as he explains the details of the renovations as we follow him on his mini tour.

Every detail is a new point of pride for him—the fresh coat of stain on the floorboards, the framed family photos on the wall, and his true pride and joy, a bar he built out of scrap metal and leftover pallets. Behind it, three stacked shelves boast a dozen or so growlers and a row of carboys where the next batch is fermenting.

"Everything's stored up here." Graham shoots me a knowing look. "So nobody can knock anything over."

The memory of the war I started with him over spilled beer puts a rotten feeling in my gut. "Again, I'm really sorry about that," I mumble, fisting my hands. I'm half ready for another fight about it, but Graham is shockingly calm.

"If you hadn't done that, I never would've come up with the design for this bar," he says plainly, turning toward the shelf of amber-tinted growlers. "So, apology accepted."

He runs his fingers along the shelf, squinting at the makeshift labels he's made with painter's tape and permanent marker. Finally, he lands on a jug that I think is labeled SHANDY. Or maybe it says SHAMU. The Tate boys have never been known for our good handwriting.

"Here. This is one I think you're gonna like,

Summer."

Reaching for a pint glass, he pours himself a taste first, swirling the buttery-yellow liquid around his glass before taking a sip. "Yeah, you're gonna like that one." He grabs a second glass and tilts the growler, pouring two fingers' worth of liquid gold. "Try that. It's fruitier than our other beers."

Summer folds her arms over her chest, popping one hip out to the side. "So, you're assuming that just because I'm a girl, I like fruitier beer?"

"No, I'm assuming that because of the face you made drinking out of the flask of whiskey the other night."

"Fair, fair," she says with a laugh, accepting the glass.

Graham and I both watch her closely as she brings it to her lips, sipping and smacking her lips the same way Graham did. Her cheeks flush an adorable shade of peach as she swallows, a glimmer twinkling in her eyes.

"Wow, you're right. That's fantastic." She holds up the glass, swirling what's left of her tasting. "I would easily pay ten bucks for a pint of that at any Boston bar."

"Really?" Graham's chest puffs up with pride.

"That means a lot."

"Here, Logan. Try it."

Summer hands me the glass, and I down the rest of it in one swallow. It's easily as good as, if not better than, any of the fancy craft beers the guys are always bringing to team get-togethers.

"Damn, dude. She's not kidding. That's good as fuck."

A wide smile breaks out across my brother's face. I haven't seen him smile like that since before we lost Dad.

"Now just think of how much better it'll be when you finally let me buy you those pricey fermenter tanks," I say.

He responds with an exaggerated scoff, but unlike every other time I've mentioned it, he doesn't immediately shoot down the offer. I may actually convince my stubborn brother to let me do something nice, not just for him, but for our whole family.

Before I can push the point any further, he selects another growler from the shelf and unscrews the lid, topping off Summer's glass with a fresh pour of a slightly darker beer.

"I have to know what you think of the IPA. Are

the hops too much?"

She takes a small sip and her eyes widen. "Oh, that's yummy."

I chuckle and watch as my normally stoic brother basically melts under her attention.

Summer takes another sip, savoring the flavors on her tongue. "Do you grow the hops here?"

Graham nods, clearly proud of this fact. "We sure do. The two main elements of beer that you can grow yourself are grains and hops. Barley is probably the most popular of the grains, and it does provide a base flavor for the beer, but hops are where it's at."

"Oh?" she asks, enjoying another sip.

"Yeah, hops are what give beer a distinct, complex bitter flavor. Plus, it's a natural preservative, which was why it was added to beer in the first place."

I try not to gape at Graham. Those are probably the most words I've ever heard my brother string together at one time.

"But if you really want to get fancy with your brewing process, you can add fresh herbs from the garden, fruit, and other edibles to create new flavors."

Summer grins. "So you're telling me CBD beer could become a thing?"

Graham leans one hip against the table, nodding. "It absolutely could. Beers are pretty versatile already with their flavor profiles, but I was thinking more along the lines of orange or grapefruit or even raspberry."

"Raspberry?" Summer makes a pleased sound at the idea of a raspberry infused beer. "You know . . . another thing you could look into to monetize your beer-making is to create take-home beer-brewing kits. People like to grow something with their own two hands. Harvest it. Make something out of it. You know?"

Graham's smile widens. "That's actually a great idea. Thanks, Summer."

"You could supply them with all the seeds, soil, little planting pots . . ." Summer ticks off these items on her fingers while Graham nods along at her brilliance.

While Graham and Summer talk marketing ideas, I join my other brothers over by the picnic table. Austen is nursing a tall glass of amber ale while Matt is dusting off his rusty guitar-playing skills, alternating between strumming chords and adjusting the gold tuning knobs.

"Are you taking requests?" I ask.

Matt shakes his head. "Nah, man. I'm the one who has a request for you."

I frown. "What are you talking about?"

He and Austen exchange a knowing look, both of them smirking like a couple of idiots. "I'd like to *request* that you make sure Summer doesn't set foot outside of Lost Haven."

As if on cue, Summer's laughter bubbles up from the other side of the barn. It's sweet and vibrant, like a sip of that shandy, and just as intoxicating.

"Why?"

Matt's eyebrows jump up and down his forehead suggestively. "I think you know why."

"Dude. Stop trying to hook up with my counselor. It's not funny." I wince at the memory of those comments he made about her on our hunting trip.

"Not what I meant," he grunts. "Quit acting like you're not insanely into her. Anyone in a two-hundred-mile radius could see that you are."

I turn toward Austen, who is nodding along with every word Matt says. My stomach twists in my gut. I guess I haven't built my walls as high as I thought.

"So what if I am?" I grumble.

"So, don't let her get on a plane." Matt levels me with a stern look. "Listen, man. This is the chillest I've ever seen you. But it's not just you. When's the last time you saw Graham this happy? Not to mention the way Mom and Grandpa are completely smitten." He looks to Austen, who shrugs, not denying this. "Just saying. I think this girl has some magical healing powers or something."

"Or maybe Mom has been slipping us all CBD again," I say. The comment earns me a laugh, but it's not enough for Matt to drop the subject.

"I'm just saying. Summer is amazing. I think you should hang on to her."

"Hang on to her? She's my counselor, dude. My shrink. Not my girlfriend."

"Yeah?" He turns his head toward the bar.

I follow his gaze to Summer, who is sipping beer and staring at me, all flirty and doe-eyed. When I catch her gaze, she smiles a little, then blinks away, pretending to be distracted.

"Is that how most shrinks look at their clients?" Austen points out. "I think not."

They drop the conversation when Summer comes sauntering our way with good news.

"Guess what? Graham is going to name a beer after me!"

"Is that so?" I lift a brow at my brother.

"The Summer Shandy," Graham says with a crooked smile. "Kind of clever, huh?"

"Well, shit," Matt says, ducking out from beneath his guitar strap. "I gotta try this Summer Shandy stat."

While the guys disappear off to the bar, Summer settles in next to me on the picnic bench, nestling a little closer to me than could be considered professional. Not that I mind. If I had it my way, she'd be cozied up in my lap. Although that would just prove Matt's point—my feelings for this girl aren't exactly subtle. Or maybe my brothers are just really good at reading me.

"You're lucky you have this, you know," she murmurs, her words soft and quiet as she rests her head on my shoulder. The beer must be getting to her.

I gesture to Graham to cut her off, and she notices, gripping my arm and giving me a playful shove. My body doesn't register that she's messing with me, though. All that clicks is that her hands are on me, tight and warm around my bicep.

Fuck, what is it about this girl that puts fire in my veins?

"Logan?"

"Hmm?" I blink out of whatever daze I momentarily slipped into.

"I said you're lucky to have this," she says again, tilting her head toward my brothers. "I know things have been hard, and that you miss your dad. But this? Your family? I'd give anything to have something like this."

There's a wistful look on her face as she takes in the happy, domestic scene around us—my brothers, laughing and teasing one another.

I clear my throat, trying to dislodge the emotion setting up shop there. "I know. I'm lucky. And I'm sorry if I've been insensitive about . . . well, everything you've been through. I know I'm a lot more fortunate than you are in the family department."

"You haven't been insensitive," she says, giving my bicep another firm squeeze.

My body responds to her touch by treating me to a kick behind my zipper. *Goddamn.* I should tell her to keep her hands to herself, but Lord knows that's the last thing I actually want.

"Honestly, you've made me feel right at home here," she murmurs. "You all have."

"So, you, uh . . ." I swallow hard, racking my brain for the right words. "You really don't have anyone back in the city?"

"No family, but I'm not sure I'd say I don't have anyone. I have plenty of friends. And Les. He's been almost like a father to me. Or a mentor, at least. He was so encouraging when I told him I wanted to start my own counseling business. Even now, I call him regularly with questions. Everything from how to change a tire to what deductions I should claim on my taxes."

The idea of Summer without anyone to look after her doesn't sit well with me. "Have you talked to him since you've been here?"

She nods, chewing nervously at her plush bottom lip. "We spoke today, actually." Her voice dips to a whisper. "He, uh, he asked me when I was coming back to Boston."

My chest constricts at the mention of her leaving.

I shouldn't be reacting this way. After all, Boston is my home too. Or at least it's where I'm living so long as I'm playing for the Titans. I've never felt at home in that city the way I feel here and now. Whether it's Lost Haven or Summer that's making me feel that way, I haven't the faintest clue.

"So, uh, what did you say?" I ask, trying and failing to sound nonchalant.

She stares down at her hands, suddenly sober as a Sunday morning. "I told him that I'm leaving tomorrow."

My heart plummets. "Why'd you say that?"

She meets my eyes. "Because it's true."

Suddenly, my throat feels like it's closing up, like I'm having an allergic reaction to the thought of her leaving. "Tomorrow?" It comes out more as a croak than a question.

"Yeah. Les has another client lined up for me. One of the team's personal trainers." She smacks a hand over her mouth, her wide brown eyes like two full moons. "Forget that I said that," she mumbles through her fingers. "That should be confidential."

"I won't say a thing."

At my promise, her worried expression fades into a soft smile. It's the only relief I can get right now.

"Thank you," she murmurs, but I can't just leave it at that. I can't let her slip away without giving her every reason to stay.

"Under one condition."

The tiniest crease forms between her eyebrows. "What's that?"

"Stay with me tonight." The words fly out of my mouth before I can stop them.

She fidgets a little, scooting a half inch away from me, and I miss her touch the second it's gone. "You know I can't do that, Logan."

Her lips form a small, sad smile, her eyes brimming with pity. I don't know if it's for me or for herself. Maybe a little bit of both. And if I stare into those eyes too much longer, I'll fall right in.

"Well then. At least let me walk you back to your cabin."

I shove up to my feet, offering her a hand. She places her palm in mine, and it's not lost on me that this is the last time I'll get to do this.

Better make it count.

After saying a quick good-night to my brothers, we slip back into our coats and out into the biting night air. Poor Summer starts shivering instantly, but it doesn't stop her from blabbering on about how fantastic Graham's operation is.

"That shandy really is spectacular," she says enthusiastically, squeezing my hand as we walk past the infamous chicken coop and toward the cabins. "And the whole barn is so beautiful. Can't you just imagine people coming in from the city? You know, stay at the cabins, go to the brewery. People would love it."

"People like you?" I ask.

She blushes again, toying with a loose strand of caramel-colored hair that's blowing around her face. "I've certainly enjoyed my stay here, if that's what you mean."

What I mean is *will you come back and never, ever leave?* But that seems a little aggressive. So I say instead, "We'll be ready whenever you decide to come back."

"We?" She pauses, assessing me with dark, inquisitive eyes. "Aren't you headed back to Boston too?"

"Yeah, soon," I say, because I'm not ready to discuss the idea that I might want to stick around here more permanently. "For now, I think I'm going to be splitting my time when I can. Fly out here during the off season and holidays and all that." I pause, kicking the gravel with the side of my boot before adding, "Maybe you could join me."

"We're not all hockey players," she reminds me. "Owning my own business means my paid time off is nonexistent. And last I checked, there aren't a whole lot of athletes that need counseling in Lost Haven."

I raise the hand that's not laced with hers. "There's at least one."

She laughs, and it warms me up quicker than a beer around a bonfire.

Two weeks ago, this girl was a total stranger. An unwelcome guest in my family home. And here we are, our fingers laced so tightly together that you'd think we'd never let go. And maybe we're not supposed to. Maybe whatever we have will transfer back to Boston.

A guy can dream, right?

"Well, this is my stop," she says, pulling me from my daydream.

We're already back at her cabin. But I don't want the night to be over, especially not if she was serious about leaving tomorrow.

"I guess it is," I grumble, cursing myself for not walking slower.

I don't want her to go. Not into her cabin, and not back to Boston. But I have no right asking her to stay.

Heaving out a sigh, I run my thumb along her soft, sensitive palm one last time. "Have a good night, Summer. I'll see you in the morning before you go?"

But several heartbeats later, neither of us has moved. We're frozen in this moment, and with every passing second, I'm slipping deeper into her chocolate-colored eyes.

Should I say something? Do something? Beg her again to come back to my cabin and to never leave my side?

God, even in my head I sound so desperate.

Before I can get a word in edgewise, Summer grips my jacket pulls me into her, knocking all the doubt right out of me. She presses up onto her toes and, without even looking around to see if anyone is watching, seals her lips to mine in a kiss so hot, it could set the cabin behind us aflame.

I push my fingers into her soft hair, sweeping my tongue over her bottom lip. It's freezing out here, but the heat sparking between each kiss warms me from the inside out. I hardly notice the cold. It's just me and her, kissing until we're breathless.

When she pulls away, I bring my hand to her cheek, tracing the flush that's creeping across her face and down her chest. I want to kiss every square inch of her sweet pink skin.

"Maybe you could come in for just a minute. You know, to warm up," she says in a small voice, as though it's just a casual offer.

But we both know better. If I step through her door, every potential version of this evening will end the same—with me tangled up with her until morning.

"Are you sure?"

But she doesn't respond. Instead, she hauls me close again, sealing her warm mouth to mine. That's all the *yes* a man could ever need.

Inside the cabin, we're out of our coats in record time, tumbling back onto her bed like we've done this dozens of times. And in my head, we have. I've played out this moment so often while lying awake in bed at night. Usually with my hand inside my boxers.

But this is real. I'm really here, in Summer's bed, fully mesmerized as she peels out of her heather-gray sweater and shimmies off her skin-tight black jeans.

She's a vision in the flickering firelight, which casts shadows that dance along her pale stomach and the curve of her hips. It's not the first time I've seen her in next to nothing. The hot springs did me that favor, back when I was dead set on looking but not touching.

But not tonight. This is the last night I have her here, and I'm tossing every rule into the fire. Tonight, we're diving headfirst into the flames.

Her eager mouth finds mine right away. Even though her hand rubbing against the front of my jeans is more than a little distracting, I want tonight to be all about her. If this is all we get, just one night together, all I want in the world is to make her feel good.

"Logan." Her voice is a breathy whimper.

I smile against her skin.

Not to worry, sweetheart. I'm going to give you everything you need.

Gently, I ease the soft cotton of her panties down, my mouth instantly watering at the sight of all the slick, hot velvet beneath. With a shift of my weight, I'm between her thighs, teasing her with kisses on my way to her most sensitive spot. She responds with a quiver, and the sting of her finger-nails sinking into my shoulders is more bliss than pain. She has her grip on me, and fuck, do I like it that way.

I test a few strokes of my tongue, savoring my name on her lips, first in low, breathy exhales, and eventually on long, sultry moans. I could get addicted to that sound if she gave me the chance. I hum my approval into her heat, memorizing her taste just in case I never get to enjoy it again.

"Logan, please," she begs on a ragged breath.

I can barely hear her over the sound of the blood pounding in my ears. Then her spine arches off the bed, saying more than words ever could. She's so sexy, so responsive to every touch of my tongue to her skin.

As her breath gets more rhythmic, so do I, finding just the right pace to stroke her as I suck her sweet flesh. With a gasp and a final shudder, I usher her right over the edge.

Watching her come is the most beautiful sight in the world. Which is why watching her leave is going to shatter me.

• • •

"Is she really going to go? Even in all this snow?" My mother eyes me from behind her coffee mug, utterly failing to hide her disappointment.

I didn't want to be the one to break the news of Summer's departure plans, but when she never showed up for breakfast this morning, someone had to say something. And that someone is obviously me.

"She's packing now," I mutter into my coffee, letting the bitter black liquid chase away the bitter feelings I'm having this morning. "So, once the weather clears, yes. One of us will have to drive her to the airport."

Just saying it out loud feels like a punishment. Leaving Summer's bed this morning was one of the hardest things I've ever had to do. I can only imagine watching her leave the state will be a million times harder.

"All the way to the airport? In this?" Mom sweeps a hand through the air, gesturing out the window.

Last night's rogue snowflakes quickly became the first full-blown snowstorm of the season, leaving all of Lost Haven tucked beneath a thick blanket of white. I'm not sure if it's a sign of a fresh start or an ominous good-bye to the woman who changed everything by stumbling, not only into my life, but into my family.

"And you don't want her to go, do you?" The way Mom says it makes it sound so simple, as though just wanting something is enough to make it true.

It doesn't matter what I want.

"Her life is in Boston."

Even I'm annoyed by how flat and lifeless my voice is, but I'm sticking to the facts this morning. No feelings, no wants. Just the truth. And the truth is that before the sun sets tonight, all that will be left of Summer is the tire tracks she'll leave in the snow.

"But it seems like she just got here." Mom pouts, swirling her spoon in loopy infinity signs through her coffee, which is really more creamer than anything else. .

"You know I have to go back soon too, right?"

She rolls her eyes, waving off the very suggestion like a foul smell. "Yes, but you have to go back. She doesn't."

The reminder is a punch to the chest. I remember our conversation from last night about how Summer doesn't get an off season like I do.

Mom's right. I'm under contract. It's two flights and an hour-long drive up the mountains just to get here. The odds of Summer making it back to Lost Haven with her work schedule are slim to none.

"Her life is in Boston," I say again through clenched teeth, silently reviewing the anger management techniques Summer taught me. I'm supposed to count down from ten.

Nine.

Eight.

Seven.

"But no, I don't want to let her go." The words come out before I can wise up enough to stop them.

Fuck it. This is how I feel, and if I can't discuss it with my own mother, then who can I discuss it with?

"Then don't let her," Mom whispers, squeezing my hand. "It's obvious you like her. Tell her how you feel."

"She knows how I feel. But she has a job back in Boston, and so do I. I'll be back there in a month."

Mom's stirring gets faster. "A lot can happen in a month."

"She's not going to fall for someone else in a

month, Mom."

"Really? Because you fell for her in less than two weeks."

Shit. She has a point.

With a shrug, Mom presses up from the table, leaving me to marinate in this weird cocktail of worry and hope. "Summer isn't the kind of girl who will stay single forever, honey. That's all I'm saying."

Just the thought makes me want to put my fist through a wall.

18

SUMMER

The blank line on the return-to-work form stares back at me, as white as the snow piled up outside the cabin window. I've been staring at these forms for the past hour, waiting for the storm to let up, and now I can barely see straight.

I, Summer Campbell, certify that Logan Tate is suited to return to work, and is ready and able to perform the functions of his position.

The words are all right there, plain and simple. All I have to do is sign my name.

The counselor in me knows that we've barely scratched the surface of Logan's issues, but the romantic in me knows that if I stay here in Lost Haven any longer . . . well, I think last night is all the evidence I need that whatever is happening between Logan and me is the furthest thing from professional.

I told him I'm leaving today. So, why can't I just work up the courage and sign my name to the paperwork that makes it official?

Les is right. I flew all the way out here and convinced Logan to do some counseling sessions with me. That was my job, and I did it. As for digging deep and really getting to the heart of his psychological issues, I did my best. It's time to close this client file before I fall in love with the man. Although admittedly, it might be too late for that.

With a heavy sigh, I uncap my pen and do what I have to. One quick scribble across the page, and the deed is done. Signed, sealed, and now I just have to deliver it. Which means hopping on a plane and taking it back to Boston where I belong. Far away from Lost Haven, and far away from Logan.

Just thinking about him, about last night, makes my head spin.

Who falls for a guy in less than two weeks? Even worse, what kind of counselor falls for her client? And why don't I feel more guilty about it than I do?

This whole situation is enough to give me a pounding headache, which is the last thing I need right now. I stare at the paper, trying to focus my attention to make the pain go away.

In any other situation, I'd be proud to sign these papers. I just successfully gave professional counseling to one of hockey's top athletes. Instead, it feels like the end of a chapter of my life that I'm not sure I'm done living. Whether I'm ready to say good-bye or not, I've got a flight to catch.

Packing is quick work, considering I only brought a few days' worth of clothes. Fitting in the new socks and toiletries from the general store, along with the small collection of gifts I've ac- crued from the family, is a bit of a challenge, but I manage to squeeze it all in. I top the bag off with the tin of tea that Jillian gave me as a parting gift. As if leaving weren't hard enough, losing Logan's family too is just the cherry on top of an ice cream sundae of suckiness.

My duffel bag's zipper snags when I try to tug it closed, and I blink back frustrated tears. I know I'm in rough shape when the smallest inconve- nience starts the waterworks. I manage to wrestle it closed with a huff. Lacing up my boots, I try as hard as I can not to think about where they came from, who bought them for me, and all the warm, fuzzy emotions attached to those memories.

Ripping a page out of my notebook, I jot down

a quick message.

Decided to brave the storm. I'll text when I'm back in Boston. Thanks for everything.

For a second, I consider writing a separate note specifically for Logan's eyes only, but I decide against it. Why make this harder than it needs to be?

I don't really have a plan when I step out into the snow, carrying my laptop bag and my duffel bag slung over my shoulder. The snowstorm has stopped, at least, so visibility will be fine on the roads. The snow itself has piled over a foot high, but this is Colorado. It snows like this every other day, from what I understand. The snowplow guys must be experts at getting the roads clear in no time, right?

Before I can psych myself out, I trudge the hundred or so yards back to the house and around it to the driveway. With one great heave, I toss my duffel into the truck bed, peering over my shoulder to make sure the noise didn't grab the attention of anyone inside. The last thing I need before I leave is to make a scene.

I tug on the door handle, and naturally, it's locked.

No, Summer, the last thing you need before you

leave are the damn truck keys.

I dig through my pockets but come up empty-handed. I must have left the set that Jillian gave me in my cabin, which I locked behind me already. But I know there's a spare set on the hook near the back door of the house.

It's easy enough to sneak back into the foyer and grab what I need. What's harder is the gravitational pull I feel as soon as I hear the familiar voices of the family inside, talking shop by the fireplace. I can hear Grandpa Al's soft snores from his recliner and Jillian in the kitchen, getting dinner going. And when Logan's deep, manly laugh echoes down the hall, my whole body quakes.

A very real, very scary thought occurs to me.

I could put the keys back on the hook so, so easily. Ten short steps into the living room, and I could snuggle up next to Logan on the couch, join in the laughter, and be a part of the family. All I have to do is put the keys back.

Instead, I shove the keys in my coat pocket and rush out the door. I don't even try to be quiet. I need to get out of here before my overactive imagination causes me any more problems.

Hopping into the truck, I replay the memory of Logan teaching me how to drive a stick shift. His hand on my thigh, encouraging me.

Focus, Summer. Ground the clutch, put it in neutral . . .

Soon the wheels are crunching against the freshly fallen snow. The truck groans and creaks, clearly unhappy with me and my choices. It takes every scrap of patience and a few emergency prayers, but I manage to get the truck to the property line, turning where I think the road begins.

So much for clear roads.

The sun is setting just ahead, reminding me that I'm mixing dangerous situations here. Driving in the dark for the first time and in the snow? This isn't the best choice I've ever made, but it's the only one that feels right.

I pull my coat tighter under my chin and reach for the heater, cranking it all the way up. The truck sputters and coughs up nothing. *Perfect*. Looks like I'll be freezing for the next hour.

Maybe it's the cold, or maybe it's because I'm finally off of the Tate property, but my feverish thoughts begin to clear.

What am I doing? What if I can't get the truck all the way to the airport? What if I get stranded out here when the sun goes down and have no way to keep warm? What if no one knows I'm gone and I freeze to death?

Flashes of me, blue-lipped and shivering in the middle of nowhere, fill my mind. I'm such a fool. I should turn back. I should never have—

The front left tire hits a big bump hidden by the snow, rocking this old rust bucket to the side. I whip the wheel to the right, trying to realign the wheels, but they don't respond. Instead, in one horrifyingly real moment, the truck slides off the road straight toward the drainage ditch.

A scream bursts from me as the truck dips into the ditch with a thud, knocking me against the steering wheel with the force of it.

Once I catch my breath, I struggle to change gears, putting the truck into reverse, and slam my foot on the gas, pleading with fate to throw me a bone. Instead, what I get is spinning tires, gaining no traction in the snow and mud. I try again and again and again, tears welling in my eyes.

What am I supposed to do? I'm nowhere near the airport, and who knows how far from the cabin I am.

In a moment of desperation, I put the truck in neutral and climb out, stumbling down a few feet into the muck to try to push the heap of metal out with brute strength. But I'm not built like a hockey player. I'm built like a damn hockey stick.

Well. I'm officially stuck.

I climb back into the truck, shivering in my now waterlogged clothes. With shaking hands, I pull out my phone to confirm what I already expected—no signal. Classic Lost Haven.

Numb inside and out, I turn off the truck and lay my head against the wheel. Tears fall steadily down my cheeks, and for the first time since I arrived here, I'm really, truly, utterly alone. And thank God I am, because there's no one to hear me cry.

I let it all out—all the anger, the frustration, the sadness, and let myself completely fall apart.

• • •

I don't know how long I sit there before I hear the faint crunch of footsteps in the snow. I look up and over my shoulder, momentarily blinded by a flashlight shining through the back window.

Which is worse, freezing to death, or getting murdered by some lunatic who preys on women stranded on country roads? I haven't yet decided when a familiar voice calls my name.

"Summer?"

Logan's deep, gravelly voice fills me with the sweetest relief I've ever felt.

Whipping the door open, I half fall out of the truck and into his arms. He crushes me against his chest, those bulky arms holding me closer than anyone has ever held me. I breathe him in, letting his warmth spread through my freezing limbs. When we finally pull apart, he cups my cheek and looks down at me, his eyes brimming with worry and hurt.

"Are you okay?" he asks, scanning my face and body, checking for injuries. Knowing someone cares this much about my well-being is like a drug.

"I'm okay," I say as I sniffle. "Just dumb."

"You're not dumb," he says firmly, correcting me. "You just did a dumb thing. There's a difference. Come on, let's get you out of the cold."

"What about the truck?"

"The guys and I will come and get it tomorrow morning. Believe me, no one is trying to drive down these roads tonight. Well, except for you. What was your plan, anyway? To leave the truck in the airport parking garage?"

I wipe some snot from my nose, laughing

through the tears. "I'm so sorry, Logan. I wasn't thinking."

"It doesn't matter," he says softly, tucking a strand of hair behind my ear. "We can talk more when we're back home. Let's get you there soon before you freeze."

Home. The word wraps around me like a blanket, and I realize just how fitting it is. Lost Haven really has become home. A home I was trying to run away from. But I guess one more night can't hurt.

Logan reaches into the bed of the truck and pulls my duffel bag out with one strong arm, and I grab my laptop bag from the passenger seat. He offers me the other arm to lean on as we make the trek back to the cabin. I didn't make it very far, turns out, so the walk isn't too bad, especially with Logan's giant footsteps paving the way. We don't talk, but I can feel a very important conversation brewing between us.

Logan leads me back into my cabin and gets to work building a fire. Once it's roaring, I stand just inches away from the woodstove, letting its radiant heat begin to defrost me.

"Here, take this," Logan says, and I turn around to see him holding out a thick wool sweater. "Your clothes are soaked."

"Thanks."

I fumble with the zipper of my coat, my fingers frozen and barely functional. After a few moments of watching me struggle, Logan intervenes.

"Can I help?"

"Yes," I say softly, and he pulls down the zipper of my jacket inch by inch. The whole time, I stare into his eyes, trying to read the dark expression on his face.

"What are you thinking?" I ask him, tilting my head to the side.

He meets my eyes for a second before peeling the coat off of my shoulders and kneeling in front of me to unlace my boots. "Come on, let's get you out of these clothes. Then you can tell me why you were trying to steal my grandfather's truck."

Unexpectedly, I laugh. "I wasn't trying to steal it. I guess I thought I'd call from the airport, and someone could come pick it up once I was in the air."

"You really didn't want to see me before you left, huh? Didn't want to say good-bye?"

My heart squeezes painfully in my chest. I open

my mouth to answer, but say nothing. What can I possibly say?

"Let's just get you changed into something warmer. Then we can talk," he says gruffly before standing and walking to the opposite side of the cabin to pour himself a drink. He keeps his back turned, either to give me some privacy or because he can't even look at me. Probably both.

I look down at my wet pants and socks and slowly peel them off, then pull the wool sweater on over my head. It's so big that it brushes against my bare knees. Even better, it smells just like him.

"All done," I say meekly. As I step up behind him, he turns, chewing on a smile he tries to hide when I wave to him, my hands drowning in fabric. "It's just my size."

"You're still shivering," he says, stepping toward me and offering me his drink, some dark amber liquid, then he wraps a fleece blanket around my shoulders.

I accept the drink and take a sip. Whiskey. He laughs a little at the way I wince.

"I should've brought your namesake shandy instead," he says coyly as I cough away the sting of the liquor. "You all right?"

"I'm okay," I assure him, reaching out to take his big, rough hand. "I'm sorry for causing all of this trouble."

"I don't understand why you would just leave like that."

The hurt in his voice almost breaks my heart in two. I never, ever want to hurt this man again. I close the space between us, close enough to feel his breath.

"I thought it would be easier," I whisper as a stray tear runs down my cheek.

"For who?"

"For me."

Logan surges toward me, capturing my mouth with his in a kiss unlike any we've shared so far. Our past kisses couldn't possibly hold a candle to this one. This kiss—this *incredible* kiss—tastes like devotion and desperation. I can't get enough of it.

Pressing onto my tiptoes, I wrap my arms around his neck just as he grabs my hips, yanking me against him with a growl. When his tongue brushes mine, I sigh into his mouth, all memory of the cold replaced by the fire of our touch.

What was life like before I stepped into Lost

Haven? I can't even remember.

"Logan," I whisper against his lips between open-mouthed kisses.

His hands trail a path down my hips and over my ass to grasp my bare thighs, lifting me into the air and pressing me flush against him. Locking my ankles behind him, I chase the sensation building between my legs by grinding against the hard muscles of his abdomen.

With a groan, Logan lowers us onto the bed, and soon he's pulling off the very sweater he tried so hard to get me into.

We can't fight this anymore . . . that much is obvious.

One by one, our clothes fall to the floor in a heap. The fire crackles faintly in the background, overpowered by the hammering of my own heart. Logan sits back to unbutton his jeans, surveying my naked body beneath him. He looks at me like he owns me, one hand running possessively down my body from my neck to my pelvis.

I squirm beneath him, eager to finally feel all of him inside me. But Logan has other plans in mind, leaning down to kiss me hard on the mouth before kissing and nipping a trail of kisses over my breasts, my belly, and finally, between my legs.

"God, Summer. Fuck," he murmurs between adoring kisses to my clit.

I buck like a wild animal beneath him, moaning his name like it's the only word I remember. It may as well be with the way his mouth is replacing every thought, every worry with pure, unmitigated pleasure.

When Logan resurfaces, his mouth is slick, and I watch with hungry eyes as he tugs off his jeans, reaches into a back pocket to grab a condom, and rolls it over his length, which is *wow*—impressive. Our eyes lock, but this time there's no uncertainty between us.

We want this. There's no stopping us now.

Logan sinks into me with one long, slow thrust. I press my face into his neck, my body shuddering in pleasure.

He murmurs sweet words, telling me how perfect I feel. The tilt of his hips is perfect, but the pace is maddening. It's like he wants to feel every inch of me around him. When I can't take it anymore, I urge him with my hips until Logan is fucking me truly, deeply.

It doesn't take long for the tension between my legs to boil over, and soon I'm gasping through an orgasm that has me seeing stars. Logan moans into my ear, leaning over me as he rocks through his own release.

We lie there in a sweaty heap, catching our breath. Now would be the time for reality to catch back up with me, but all I can manage is to curl into his side and press lazy kisses against his shoulder. A smile twitches on his lips, and he sighs with total satisfaction.

Now all we need is for tomorrow to never come.

19

LOGAN

Sunlight filtering through the front windows wakes me, and a smile lifts my lips when I open my eyes. Summer is still beside me. She's curled on her side, facing away from me, and I roll closer, tugging her warm body next to mine.

"Hey," she says sleepily.

"You awake?"

"Sort of," she murmurs, stretching and relaxing into me.

"How'd you sleep?" I ask, holding her close.

"Amazingly. Although I gotta say, I didn't know you were the cuddling type."

I chuckle. "I didn't either."

The truth is, I've never been the cuddling type

before Summer. But the few times I woke up, I was happy to realize I wasn't alone, that she was still in bed, warm and softly breathing beside me. I moved closer and held her then, thankful for her presence.

Resting my palm on her waist, I bring my lips to hers and give her a soft kiss. She wraps her arms around me, pressing closer, and I wonder if she can tell I'm hard. Although it's not because I was having indecent thoughts about waking up with her this morning . . . I'm like this every morning. But now that she's kissing me back, my body gets a bunch of new ideas about how we can make the most of our morning. I refuse to think about the fact that it could be our last morning together.

Matt's words ring in my head. *Find a way to make her stay.*

Summer pulls back and meets my gaze with a shy expression. Her hair is loose on the pillow, messy from sleep. *Damn, she's gorgeous.* Even having just woken up, without a bit of makeup on.

"Thanks for letting me stay," I say, pressing my lips to her shoulder. "Last night was incredible."

This time with her has been so much more than I was expecting. She's so low-drama and sweet. My entire family has fallen in love with her. There's that l-word again. I can't seem to help myself from it constantly flitting through my brain, which is completely out of character for me.

I'm about to ask her if she wants to get up, maybe get some coffee, or even pancakes in town at a great diner I know, when Summer trails her fingertips over my chest, then down over the muscles in my stomach. My pulse jumps, and I forget all about breakfast.

The press of her soft curves fitting against me sends a jolt of desire down my spine.

While her hand ventures under the elastic of my boxer briefs, I begin exploring too, testing the weight of her luscious breasts in my palms. Finally, I draw her panties down her legs.

A few minutes later, when I join us, her breath catches in her throat. It's the best sound, so desperate and need-filled. Of the two of us, she's the strong one, the one with her life together. She was sent here to help *me*—and here she is coming undone for me. I love it.

"You feel so *fucking* good, sweetheart," I growl, picking up the pace.

She moans and clutches my hips in her hands to draw me even closer.

Our lovemaking is slow and unhurried, and

completely perfect.

Which is why, when Summer is showered and had coffee, I'm shocked when she walks out of the bedroom carrying her bags.

The crunch of tires in the driveway catches our attention, and I look through the window to see a yellow minivan parked in front of the cabins. The sign on the side of the van advertises rides to the airport.

My neck feels hot, and when I turn to face Summer, everything inside my brain scrambles. "Sweetheart?"

"I called a shuttle service to pick me up."

I give her an uncertain look. "You . . ."

She nods. "I didn't want to inconvenience anyone by asking for a ride. But I need to get back to the city. It's time."

My chest throbs with the displeasure of that statement, and I rub at the tender spot unconsciously. Even though everything inside me disagrees with it, I give her a stiff nod and cross the room to help her with her bag.

Her duffel has grown considerably heavier since she's been here. A stack of books that my mother insisted she take. A new pair of boots. A wool scarf that Grandpa Al loaned her and made her promise to keep. Then there's the piece of my heart she's taking with her . . . does she even know?

I swallow a painful lump in my throat as Summer opens the cabin's door and waves to the driver. A gust of frigid air sweeps over us.

She turns to face me, but before she can tell me good-bye, I take her hands and squeeze.

"I don't want you to go."

The words are real, and raw, and I watch as Summer draws a quiet breath.

"It's been amazing being here, Logan, but I—"

"Can't you stay . . . even a few more days?" I pause, weighing my words. "We should talk about this thing with us."

This *thing*. The word is entirely wrong for the depth of emotions I've experienced these past couple of weeks.

With a sad look, Summer shakes her head. "I can't stay. I can't be with you like this. It would be a huge conflict of interest, and my entire professional reputation would be shot. It's all I have."

"Summer . . ." I caress the back of her hand with my thumb. She can't just walk away from something this big.

"I'm sorry. I can't. No matter how much I might want to." Her hand slips from my grasp.

"Would it change things if you were married? I mean, no one could hold anything against you if your husband just happens to play hockey, right?"

The stunned look on her face is priceless. I just shocked her, but I won't apologize for thinking big, crazy thoughts. Marrying Summer would be crazy, but also . . . well, *perfect*.

When her shock fades away and is replaced by cool indifference, I know I'm not that lucky.

"No, I guess not."

"Then marry me." The words fall from my mouth without warning, without grace.

I'm not down on one knee, and I don't have a ring, but there's a sincerity in my words. An absolute truth. And isn't that what she's wanted from me this entire time—facing my truth, letting myself be vulnerable? It doesn't get any more vulnerable than this. I brush my fingertips against her cheek, tilting her face to mine.

Summer blinks. "I can't . . . I can't just marry you."

My stomach lurches. "Why not?"

"Because . . ."

20

SUMMER

Because.

The word hangs between us as my mind goes blank.

Logan blurted out a marriage proposal without even thinking. Of course I can't hold him to it. But he's still watching me, and despite the intensity of our connection, there's no way I can marry him.

But why not?

I'm falling in love with him. And with his big meddling family. Isn't this everything I've ever wanted?

Of course it is. Say yes, my brain pleads.

"I just can't," I say after a long beat of silence.

"Okay," he says softly and releases my hands.

The shuttle driver steps out of the minivan and comes around to help with my bags, seemingly oblivious to the enormity of the moment he's interrupting.

Ignoring him, Logan pulls me close for one last hug, causing a sharp ache to pierce my chest.

"Good-bye, Summer," he whispers against my hair.

"Good-bye, Logan."

• • •

I held myself together for the entire shuttle ride, all the way through airport security and for ninety percent of the flight from Durango to Denver. But there's something about this second flight, the one from Denver back to Boston, that feels different. More final.

As I buckle my seat belt in my lap and pull it tight, the last of the mountain air deflates from my lungs. This is it. I'm going home. And to be totally honest, I'm feeling about a hundred different ways about it.

For one, I'm proud. At least a little, I think. After all, I did what I set out to do—I helped Logan. Maybe it didn't happen how I expected, but the man I left back at the cabin is so different from the one I met when I arrived in Lost Haven.

He's calmer now, more in touch with his feelings and how to deal with them in a healthy way. Mission accomplished, as far as counseling goes, which means it's time to head home. Back to Boston and back to my normal life, where I don't have to sit through violent dinner table arguments or psychoanalyze an entire family of brothers with broken pasts.

Things will be easier back home. Just me, my studio apartment, and my work. The way it's always been.

And that's where pride ends and depression sets in. Because maybe the way it's always been isn't what I want anymore.

My throat prickles, but I wrestle the tears down as best I can. I've made it this far without crying in public. Maybe I can make it home before I fully break down.

Swallowing hard, I focus on the flight attendant's demonstration. She buckles and unbuckles a seat belt, pivoting so that everyone onboard can see, but hardly anyone is paying much attention.

The two other people in my row, a mother and her teenage son, aren't even pretending to listen.

They both have earbuds in, each of them bobbing their heads to their own preferred playlist. When one of the boy's earbuds falls out, his mom reaches over and tucks it back into his ear, and he gives her the sort of half smile that tells me it's far from the first time this has happened.

Of course, they remind me of Logan and his mom, and the prickling feeling climbs up my throat to my nose until the tears push past my eyelids. Jesus, I should have gotten this out on the tiny bi-plane from Durango to Denver. At least then there wouldn't be an audience to witness my sobs.

I turn toward the window, fixing my gaze on the wing of the plane as the tears start falling steadily. Soon, the sleeve of my cardigan is wet with tears and snot, and all I can do is pray that my seat part-ners have their earbuds in tight. It's not like me to cry in public like this, but then again, it's not like me to fall in love with one of my clients either.

And that's what I did, isn't it? I fell in love with Logan Tate. Faster than I thought was humanly possible and harder than I thought my heart could handle.

And maybe I can't handle it. Maybe that's why I ran off so fast. Maybe I thought that would be easier somehow. I know now that I was wrong. I'll miss the smell of a wood-burning stove and Logan's winter-air scent.

The plane rumbles beneath me, and I realize the flight attendant has wrapped up her presentation and taken her seat, ready for takeoff. I must have missed the part where they tell us to turn our phones to airplane mode.

Reaching into my carryon, I grab my phone and swipe it open. But before I kiss my service good-bye, I open up that email from Les, scrawl my digital signature on the paperwork he sent over, and press **SEND**.

There. Logan is all set to return to the ice the second his suspension is over. And just like that, he's no longer my client. It's a thought that stirs up a strange, fluttery feeling in my chest.

If he's not my client, maybe he could be something else. Like my boyfriend or, eventually, my . . .

No. I shut that thought down quicker than I can power off my phone.

I am absolutely not allowing myself to think about Logan's insane proposal right now. It had to have been the post-sex endorphins talking, or maybe he was just living out some sort of weird domestic fantasy of his. Either way, he didn't actually mean it. And even if he did, I've known the man for all of fourteen days.

Fourteen magical, whirlwind days.

My heart swells as each one of them plays through my memory like a highlight reel. From the first time I stepped into that house, there was something about him that I was instantly attracted to. And then that night Jillian sent him to build a fire in my cabin, that's when I felt the first spark.

But this feeling in my chest now is much larger than that. It's a roaring wildfire that torched any chance I had at being professional. That was made quite clear last night . . . and again this morning.

Heat floods my system at the memory of his strong arms around me, his warm lips at my neck. Last night, I felt like I was living for the first time, not just existing. Maybe that's what a life with Logan would be like. A life worth living instead of merely going through the motions.

An ache builds deep inside me as the rumbling stops and a weightless feeling builds inside me. Takeoff. I'm officially no longer on Colorado soil. Time to leave it all behind me.

Once we reach cruising altitude, the tears subside, leaving me completely exhausted. At least it means I can sleep through this flight.

• • •

I hardly remember making the decision to sleep, but in what feels like two blinks and a yawn, the rumbling touchdown of the plane in Boston wakes me from my dream about—you guessed it—Logan. You can take the girl out of Lost Haven, but I guess you can't stop the memories from following her home.

Once we've deplaned, it's only a ten-minute cab ride back to my Southie apartment, where everything is exactly as I left it.

The coffee mug in the sink and the hamper of half-folded laundry remind me of what I thought this trip would be. A quick turnaround, no more than a day or two. Get in, persuade the client to work with me, and get out. I should have been back before the produce in my fridge went bad. It's almost a funny thought now.

Exhausted, I let my duffel drop to the hardwood with a thud that echoes through the empty apartment, reminding me that, for the first time in weeks, I am really, truly alone.

With a sigh, I set aside my laptop bag, flip on the lights, and sink into the cushions of my couch, flipping on the TV to have some background noise.

The chatter of some sitcom family instantly calms me and simultaneously revs up my imagination. I wonder what the Tates are up to tonight. Maybe Austen built a bonfire and they're cozied up around it, drinking home-brewed beer and swapping stories about growing up.

I check the time on my phone. It's early enough that they could still be eating dinner, with Jillian carving up a perfectly cooked venison roast. I'll bet they've already put away that extra chair they pulled out specially for me. The thought stings.

And then it really sets in. The loneliness. And not the usual kind, either. This is something deeper. Heavier.

For so long, I've been used to my life, my little studio apartment that I don't have to share with anyone. I reported the ins and outs of my life to my journal or social media instead of calling my mom, like my friends get to do. I was perfectly content not knowing what I was missing.

But for a short time, I had a family. Friends. A man I was hopelessly falling for. And the hollowness in my gut tells me maybe I shouldn't have left it all behind.

But it's too late now. I left. I threw away whatever precious and fragile thing we'd built. It's over.

And it's all my fault.

21

LOGAN

I head off toward the old barn at the farthest end of the property, stuffing my hands into the pockets of my coat to fight off the November chill.

Too brokenhearted and hurt to appreciate the awesome views of the mountains and frost-covered lake in the distance, I keep my head down and trudge onward.

Ever since Summer left, my head's been full of nothing but her, and my stomach has been twisted up in so many knots, I can barely eat. Even my mom's homemade lasagna, which has always been a favorite of mine, has held no appeal.

Summer made me feel things I have no use for feeling. Made me desire things I never thought I'd want. A wife. A little house of my own overlooking the valley. Kids. Maybe a dog someday. Something with a wagging tail and floppy ears that we would laugh at.

But I can't let myself think about Summer right now. Just the very thought of her affects me, causing a stir of deep longing to pulse through my veins. There's work to be done this morning, and I'm not ready to face all that I've lost at such an early hour.

I need more coffee for that. Or maybe one of those strong cocktails called a mind-eraser, despite it being barely eight in the morning.

When I reach the old barn where we store equipment, I let myself inside and am greeted by the familiar smell of diesel fuel and leather.

It'll be a busy day today, and first on the agenda is changing the oil on the snowblower. I'm grateful for the mindless work. Something to do with my hands will be good.

I haven't seen Graham yet this morning. He started his workday early, so it's not like I've been flat-out avoiding him. Although after he texted me last night saying we should talk, I was too stunned to reply. Graham isn't the talk-it-out type, so whatever is on his mind is sure to be serious. And I don't think I can handle anything else serious right now.

After locating a pair of vise-grip pliers, I get to

work removing the thumbscrew. I'm not very far into my task when the heavy barn doors open, and in with a gust of wind comes Graham.

"There you are." He frowns, coming closer.

"You found me. I'm taking care of Big Bertha."

He nods, his frown fading. It's the nickname we affectionately gave our snowblower. She's a beast, one of the last things Dad bought for the property before he passed. We all love this snowblower.

Once the screw is almost free, I set an empty paint can beneath the machine to let the old oil drain into, then remove the screw all the way.

"You wanted to talk?" I nod to Graham, who's still watching me, obviously with something on his mind.

My brothers haven't said much since Summer took off. Maybe it's a guy thing. They didn't want to pry. My mother and grandfather had no such qualms, though. They both questioned me repeatedly about what I'd done. They both assumed I'd somehow screwed things up with her.

If they only knew the truth. I asked Summer to marry me that last day. But even that wasn't enough to get her to stay. The pain of her rejection still stings deep inside.

Graham takes a seat on an empty stool beside me. "You need to go home, Logan."

I roll my eyes. "This is home."

"Not for you, it isn't. Not anymore."

I watch the last of the oil drain into the paint can, and then pull out the dipstick to be sure the reservoir is good and empty.

"You've got a shot most people would kill for. You can't fuck that up. This will always be your home, but not right now. You've got what, five, maybe ten good years to play hockey?"

I replace the dipstick and tighten the thumbscrew. "Yeah, I guess." An average NHL contract is five years.

"Exactly. Then that's what you need to be doing." Graham's tone leaves no room for negotiation.

Silence settles around us as I grab a quart of motor oil and twist off the top, then begin slowly pouring it into the machine.

"Unless you're telling me you don't like playing hockey anymore, and you'd rather hang around here listening to me bark out orders all day?"

I shrug. "Never said I don't like hockey."

"That's what I thought. And I doubt you want to spend your time reroofing the barn or harvesting the garden?"

"It's honest work."

"It is. But does the idea of listening to me bitch about the cost of new fermentation tanks appeal to you?

I chuckle. "Not exactly."

"Then go back to Boston. Your team needs you."

I consider his words. "And what about you guys?"

"We'll manage. Just like we always do."

With the oil topped off, I wipe my hands and turn to face Graham. "You really want me gone that badly?"

He scoffs. "Of course not. I want what's best for you."

There's a sincerity to his words.

"And when you retire, move back here, if you like. Build yourself a nice house on that ten acres on the other side of the river." He points his chin in the direction of the acreage I've had my eye on.

I nod. "That might be nice."

Graham agrees. "It would. It's a prime spot. Far enough away from Mom and Al to be private, but not so far that you can't easily swing by for a homecooked meal."

He has a point. But thinking about my future . . . about a future without Summer by my side? It's not something I can let myself do right now.

"One other thing," Graham says, rubbing a hand over his stubbled jaw. "When you get back to Boston, stop with the fighting. That's not what Dad would want either."

I hang my head. "Okay."

Graham clutches my shoulder and gives it a good hard squeeze. "We're all proud of you, kid. You know that, right?"

"Thanks." I break into a smile because sometimes it's just nice to hear those words. Lately, I've felt like everything I touch turns to shit.

A warm feeling rushes through me. The other thing that's surprising is the fact that these encouraging words are leaving *Graham's* mouth.

"Damn, dude, I didn't think you had it in you." I grin at him.

"Had what?"

"The patriarch thing. Giving advice. Filling in for Dad. Those are the most words I've heard you string together . . . ever."

He chuckles. "Well, who the hell knows? Maybe I'm rising to the occasion. Maybe we all will."

That's a nice thought.

"What about Mom? How's she doing?" I ask, knowing she confides in Graham more than she does the rest of us.

He pauses to consider his response. "She has good days and bad days, just like anyone else. But she'll be okay. We all will. One day at a time, right?"

"I guess so."

I toss the empty motor oil container in the trash can and fire up the snowblower to make sure it starts. After letting it run for a minute, I shut her off.

"Should we head back?" I ask.

Graham doesn't seem to be in any hurry. "There's one other thing. What happened with you and Summer?"

I inhale sharply at the mention of her name.

The dull ache in my chest gives a painful kick. "Not talking about that."

The wounds are still too fresh. It hurts too much. And I doubt that her rejection of my proposal will ever stop stinging.

Graham nods thoughtfully. "Fair enough. Every man's allowed to have one thing that's off-limits."

"Thanks."

"One other thing," he says. "You tell anyone about this little heart-to-heart chat we had, and it'll totally ruin my reputation for being an asshole."

A laugh falls from my lips. "I wouldn't dare dream of it. Your secret is safe with me."

22

LOGAN

I often think of Summer's advice to me . . . *you can't enjoy the sweet until you've tasted the bitter.*

But lately, it feels like everything in my life has turned bitter. When she left, she took any bit of leftover sweetness with her. All the softness is gone, replaced only by hard edges. All of her sunny smiles and those sweet kisses and her gentle concern . . .

But I can't focus on that right now, because I'm preparing to walk into a conference room at the Elite Airlines Stadium in Boston for a meeting with my coach.

I adjust my tie and check my watch. I'm five minutes early because Coach appreciates punctuality. See? I have learned a thing or two during my suspension.

Taking a deep breath, I wrap my hand around the doorknob, telling myself that I'll be okay with whatever happens next. Only I'm not sure that's entirely true.

When I enter the room, I find Coach Wilder seated alone at the conference table.

For a moment, I pause and blink at him. I expected there would be other people here—several members of the coaching staff, maybe that lady from player safety, perhaps even someone from the league. A tiny part of me held on to some hope that maybe Summer would be here at this meeting too. Of course, I'm not so lucky.

I built it up in my head, imagining what I might say to her if she were here. Pictured her lips tilting up in a smile at me from across the room. Thought about how it would feel to have her bright eyes directed my way again.

Those thoughts got me through the past few days. But of course she's not here, and she's not coming.

Coach Wilder, oblivious to my inner turmoil, stands and extends his hand. "Tate. Welcome back, kid. You're looking good. You feel good?"

I clear my throat. "Is it just us, or . . ."

He motions to the door just as it's opening again. In walks Les, the front office manager, and we all take our seats as Les apologizes for running late. He puts his phone on silent and then turns his attention to Coach.

Coach exhales slowly and fixes me with a concerned expression. "Well? How was your time away?"

I straighten and respond with the word my agent told me to use. "Productive."

Coach nods and his brow relaxes. "That's good to hear. And your family?"

I force myself to smile. "Everyone's doing as well as can be expected."

Coach nods again, and Les discreetly looks at his watch. This is the man Summer regards as a sort of father figure in her life, though I'm not sure he even realizes it. Part of me wonders if I should say something to him. Let him know how important his guidance has been for her, then I decide against it.

Coach taps the conference table with his knuckles. "Let's get down to it. Your therapist sent in her report, clearing you to play."

I nod my understanding and shift in my chair,

my tie suddenly too tight. "So . . . that's it? I'm good?"

Coach's eyes narrow. "You feel ready to return?"

"Absolutely."

If I'm not here to play hockey, there's no reason for me to be here in Boston at all. And if Coach thinks I'm going to grovel, then he doesn't know me very well. There's plenty to keep me busy back at home.

"Then go warm up," Coach says with a grin.

We have a game tonight, and I had no idea if I'd be playing in it or not. I guess that answers that.

"Yes, sir," I say, rising to my feet.

• • •

I had time for my entire pre-game ritual, but going through the motions felt off, like I was doing things underwater.

Tonight probably won't be my best game, but what I lack in skill, I'll make up for in determination. I wonder if Summer is aware of my return, if she'll watch tonight's game on TV. Just the idea that she might will be enough to push me.

I skated for a while before riding the stationary bike for twenty minutes to loosen up my legs, and then I stretched and grabbed a protein shake. Now I'm in the dressing room listening to one of my teammates, Lucian, announce to everyone that his wife is pregnant. There are cheers and congratulatory remarks, but inside, I feel hollow and more alone than I ever have. Knowing I don't have a wife, a baby on the way… let alone a girlfriend, after I'd come so close with Summer, is a depressing one.

Saint pauses beside me and claps a hand on my shoulder. "Good to have you back, brother."

I nod once. "Good to be back."

Saint grins at me. "Let's go have some fun."

An hour later, we take the ice. Damn, it feels good to be back. Even better than I anticipated.

My legs feel good, and I'm alert and ready. Maybe my time away was just the break I needed.

I make my way down the ice, remembering the things Summer told me. *Be ready and aware, and expect things not to go my way.* I know I won't lose my cool if they do.

In fact, when a young defenseman pushes me

up against the boards during a power play, I only laugh and skate away.

"Try harder next time!" I call out to him with a smirk. The confused look on his face is priceless.

Throughout the game, I keep my head clear and myself calm through the nerves and pressure, and in the end? We manage to pull off a win against Los Angeles, and I'm on top of the world.

After the game, my phone blows up with messages, missed calls from my mom and grandpa, and a string of texts from my brothers.

But there's nothing from Summer. It hurts more than I expected it to.

I head home to my condo, only fifteen minutes from the arena. The entire drive there, I mentally list all the reasons why I shouldn't be the one to contact Summer. I've wanted to call or text her a thousand times since she left Colorado.

But she made her feelings clear, didn't she?

The next day, I'm scheduled to fly to Toronto with the team for a series of games in Canada. I'm busy, and it's good to be back, but it's also been harder than I thought because I can't stop thinking about Summer. I can't help but wonder what she's doing. Working, maybe? Although, it's a Saturday, so for her sake, I hope not.

One thing is certain—she's not surrounded by a big, loud team or an overbearing family. She's all alone. And the idea of an incredibly sweet woman like Summer being alone doesn't sit right with me. My mom's right in thinking Summer won't stay single forever.

• • •

By the time we deplane the next day, the guys have come up with a plan.

Saint and Alex drag me off to the hotel bar with the excuse of grabbing a soda, but really, I think it's just a pretext for wanting to check up on me. Things have been busy with my return—I've jumped right in and haven't had the chance to really talk with them. Not about things other than hockey, anyway.

I have a sinking feeling I'm about to get grilled. Turns out, I'm right.

As soon as we're seated with drinks in front of us, Saint turns to me. "What's your deal, man?"

It's not the smoothest sentence that's ever been uttered, but hockey players aren't known for their sensitivity.

My eyebrows shoot up. "My deal?"

Saint shrugs. "Yeah, your . . . situation. Everything okay now?"

I relax a little, realizing his intentions are good. He's just worried about me, I guess, and this is his way of showing it. When my gaze moves to Alex, I can see the same look of worry reflected in his eyes too. It's more touching than I expected to realize my teammates have been worried about me.

For some reason, my mind snags on a memory of Summer. She told me once that I'm lucky I have so many people who care about me.

"Everything's . . ." I want to say *okay*, but the word won't come out. It gets stuck in my throat and doesn't budge. After several seconds of awkward silence, I finally manage to string a few words together. "I don't know, to be honest."

Saint nods. "That's fair."

"Your family? Your mom? How are they?" Alex asks.

I let out a slow exhale. "My dad's departure has left a huge hole in my family, and it's . . ." I pause and draw another breath. "Well, it's going to take some time."

The guys nod.

"But that's not what's bothering you?" Saint asks.

I shake my head. When did hockey players get so perceptive? "Not really, no."

They wait patiently as we sip our drinks.

"I met someone. Her name is Summer. And I . . ." It's so crazy, I can barely say the words. "I'm in love with her."

Saint's eyes widen at my unexpected announcement. "That's great. Right?"

Alex tilts his head to the side, watching me.

"She doesn't feel the same."

"Shit," Saint mutters, and I nod.

I wish I could stop thinking about her. Wish I could move on and just focus on my career and my family like I'm supposed to. My life would be so much easier if all I cared about was hockey.

Summer is the one who told me we shouldn't gloss over things. She wanted total honesty, wanted me to tell her all of it. All the ugly, messy truth. What about now? Am I supposed to call her and admit the depth of my feelings for her? Admit that I feel heartbroken and numb and awful every second of every day?

When I left Boston for Colorado, I was torn up inside with constant worry and guilt rioting through my veins. Now that I'm back and supposedly better, I'm torn up for a very different reason.

I never expected to fall in love with Summer, but that's exactly what happened.

I barely keep up with the details of the conversation happening between Alex and Saint. Apparently, there's some beef between Saint and our captain, Reeves. But to be honest, I'm too distracted to care. Why? Because I've just made the decision to visit Summer when I return to Boston.

One last time, I'll open myself up and give her my full truth. Total honesty, just like she requested of me.

I'll tell her how I feel, and if she rejects me again, then that's it. I'll move on.

23

LOGAN

It wasn't difficult to get Les to give me Summer's address, which I have mixed feelings about. He shouldn't give out her personal information, but I may have implied that I needed it for counseling purposes, so perhaps I can't blame the guy. Maybe he thought he was only doing his job.

It's a twenty-minute drive across town, and then another several minutes before I locate a parking spot. It's just after seven on a Wednesday evening. The sky is dark, and the night air is freezing as I approach her building on the sidewalk.

I'm not sure what I was expecting, but it wasn't this. Her apartment building is in an area of town I'm not familiar with, and to be honest, I don't ever want to visit again. There's a liquor store on the corner with bars in the windows. A pawn shop and a laundromat flank her building on either side. Across the street is a bail bonds storefront.

This is a rough area. I don't like the thought of Summer living here alone, no matter how affordable the rent is.

Expecting the building's front door to be locked, I press the buzzer, but it doesn't work. So I try the door, and to my surprise, it isn't locked, so I let myself into the building.

The hallway smells like tobacco and is filled with doors lining both sides. Her apartment is number eighteen, and I head up the stairs and find her door. There's a mat outside the front door with the word HOME written on it, but the O is a heart.

An unexpected pang of emotion hits me. Realizing that this is it—this little apartment is her home where she cooks and sleeps alone every night—is a sad thought. Summer deserves so much more. She deserves the world. Someone who loves her. A family to call her own…

I lift my hand and knock twice on the door, hearing footsteps approach on the other side. There's no peephole in the door, and I realize that showing up here unannounced may surprise her. And not in a good way.

I knock again. "Summer? It's Logan."

She twists the lock and the door opens. "Logan?"

The first sight of her is like a soothing balm to my soul. Her hair is loose around her shoulders, and she's wearing plaid pajama pants with a baggy T-shirt. But she's beautiful.

"Hi," is the only word I can manage.

Her brown eyes widen with surprise. "What are you doing here?"

It's been weeks since I've seen her. I've been from Colorado to Boston to Toronto to Calgary and back to Boston again. And I thought of her through every mile and in every time zone.

"This is your place," I say, rather than responding to her question. Because the total honesty that she'll want from me isn't something I'm ready to give her just yet. Maybe because the threat of rejection is still possible and very real.

She steps aside and motions for me to enter. I make my way inside, scanning the room as I take it all in. Her place is a tiny efficiency with a futon bed. It's cold, with none of the warmth or personality I would expect of her home.

"Have you lived here long? It's pretty . . . spartan."

She inhales through her nose and wanders toward the windows. "It's clean, and it's what I can afford right now."

"Of course. I'm sorry, I shouldn't have said that."

Damn, I'm already off on the wrong foot.

"It's okay," she says, turning to face me.

Her eyes have a faraway look in them, and I realize for the first time that she looks sad. It's an expression I've never seen her wear before, and I don't like it. I want to see her smile, hear her laugh. I rub at an achy spot in the center of my chest.

"Would you like to sit?" she asks, motioning to the futon sofa.

I nod, and we take a seat.

I don't know where to start, so I do the only thing I can think of. "You asked what I was doing here. Total honesty?"

Her gaze slowly meets mine, and she nods. "Always."

I inhale slowly. "When you left me back in Colorado, something inside me broke."

Confusion and maybe something hopeful flashes through her eyes. "Logan . . ."

I take her hand and press it into my palm. "Hold on. I'm not done."

She nods for me to go ahead.

"I know it scared you, but I meant every word I said to you that day you left. I've fallen for you. I think about you every second."

Summer doesn't answer, and my heart hammers uncomfortably against my ribs.

I squeeze her hand. "Summer. Say something."

"Total honesty," she says. "Yeah, it does scare me. It scares the hell out of me."

"You're not alone anymore. You know that, right? I'll be your family."

"Just you?"

"Yes." I bring her hand to my lips and press a soft kiss to it. "You can have all of me. All I want is to make you happy. To make you whole, just like you did for me."

Tears fill her eyes. "I want that too." She draws in a deep breath. "But I'm scared. What if it doesn't work out?"

I press my lips to her knuckles again and then hold her hand in my lap. "Aren't you the one who told me it's okay to be vulnerable sometimes?"

She smiles. "I guess I was. Are you thinking I need to take my own advice?"

"It was good advice. Come on, sweetheart. Take this chance with me."

"You're a hard man to say no to."

I place my fingers beneath her chin and bring her mouth to mine. Our kiss is slow, sweet, soft. When I pull back a moment later, there are unshed tears glistening in her eyes. I tug Summer into my lap, needing her close, needing to comfort her.

"I love you, Summer." My voice is thick with emotion, and hers is too when she says it back to me.

"I love you, Logan."

They're the four best words I've heard in a very long time.

"But just so you know . . . being with me comes with a big, loud family."

She laughs. "Yeah. I kinda figured that out."

"They love you, you know."

"I love them too," she says, and I know she means it. "We can spend Christmas snowed in with them?"

"Of course." I trail my hand along her spine, gently rubbing her back. Now that she's finally in my arms again, I can't seem to stop myself from touching her.

"And Thanksgiving?"

"If you like. My mom makes the best sweet potato pie in the entire world. And my brothers fight over who gets to carve the turkey."

She lifts her head from its resting place on my shoulder and meets my eyes. "Who usually wins?"

"Grandpa Al," I say with a grin.

"Of course he does. It sounds perfect."

"It is, but wherever you are will be perfect too. You're what I want. We can make our own traditions. If you want to have Thanksgiving dinner right here in this apartment, we'll do exactly that."

She glances toward her efficiency kitchen with its tiny two-burner stove. "My kitchen sucks."

I chuckle at her honesty. Her kitchen does leave *a lot* to be desired. "I'll build you a better one."

"My hero," she says wistfully, grinning at me.

I brush her hair behind her ear. "I tell you I love you, but you're more excited about me telling you I'll build you a kitchen." I raise one eyebrow in her direction.

"Sorry! No. Not *more* excited, but maybe equally excited? And I love you too. It's just that I had a lot of good times with your mother in her kitchen. I think I might like a nice kitchen of my own someday. I've never had a nice kitchen," she says quickly, babbling like she does when she's excited.

I quiet her with another kiss. "It's yours."

"I could bake you bread, and scones, and a cake on your birthday . . . They say the way to a man's heart is through his stomach."

"You already have my heart."

We kiss and hold each other on her sofa for a long time. When I finally pull back, I meet her eyes again. "You looked so sad when I first walked in."

She nods. "I was happy to see you, *so* happy. But then I realized that I couldn't put my arms around you, couldn't hug you or kiss you or touch you, and that made me so incredibly sad."

I brush my fingers along her collarbone. "Sweetheart, you can touch me as much as you want."

This makes her laugh, and it's the best sound.

"I missed you," I say, pressing my lips to the top of her head.

You can't appreciate the sweet if you never have the bitter.

And having Summer back in my arms is the sweetest thing in the world.

24

SUMMER

Two months later

There comes a moment when you know a house has become a home.

It starts as the smallest bit of warmth in your heart the second you step over the threshold, but with a little time, it spreads to your knees, then fills up the spaces between your toes.

You know it's coming when the smell of dirty work boots and dinner in the oven isn't just familiar, it's comforting, like an old sweater that still fits, or a song you forgot you knew all the words to. It's a perfect, special feeling that doesn't come around too often, a feeling I wasn't sure I'd ever get to feel again.

And then the Tate family changed all that.

The first time I stepped into this house, I was a stranger, only here for one reason—to convince a hotheaded hockey player to seek counseling. A few short months later, that hockey player isn't so hotheaded, and the list of reasons why I'm here could stretch from Lost Haven to Massachusetts.

Reason number one? I'm madly in love with him.

Reason number two? I'm meeting his extended family, all of whom have flown from different parts of the country to stay in the cabins on the Lost Haven property.

Why? Well, that would be reason number three—

Logan and I are getting married tomorrow. And sitting here, surrounded by the people who are soon to become my official family, I've never felt so at home.

"Go ahead, lovebirds! Open another present!" Jillian calls out between nibbles of a homemade currant scone.

While she promised to keep this bridal shower small, the pile of presents in the middle of the room is anything but. I've spent what feels like hours on the couch with my knee pressed against the hard muscle of Logan's thigh, each of us taking turns peeling tape and silver wrapping paper off of packages.

With each present opened, a new wonderful feeling bubbles to the surface. Pride. Joy. Complete and utter bliss. And most of all, disbelief that this beautiful life is really mine. A loving family, a sunny winter day, and in less than twenty-four hours, the promise of forever with the incredible man beside me.

"Go ahead, babe." Logan nods toward the pile of boxes and gift bags, which is still awfully big, despite the hour and a half we've been chipping away at it. "You pick the next one."

"No, you pick," I say. "I picked out the last one we opened."

"Who cares who picks!" one of Logan's cousins shouts from the kitchen, piling a plate high with what's left of the finger sandwiches. "If we don't speed up this operation, the bride will still be opening presents on the honeymoon."

Logan wraps a big, protective hand around my thigh, sparking a warm humming sensation across my skin. "No wife of mine is doing anything on our honeymoon other than sitting in her beach chair and drinking as many fruity cocktails as she can handle."

He shoots me a wink and a warm smile, but I'm too hung up on the word *wife* to respond. Just one more day until I officially take on that role, and while I don't want to wish away this precious family time, I would turn the clock forward just to make him officially mine already.

"Why don't we save some of these for tomorrow?" I say, checking the time for the first time since we sat down. It's nearly one o'clock, a full hour later than the invitations said this brunch would wrap up. The last thing I want to do is make a bad impression on my soon-to-be relatives.

"You can't open these tomorrow, silly," Jillian says. "These are *shower* presents. Tomorrow you'll have *wedding* presents. That's a whole different can of worms."

All I can do is shake my head and laugh. This isn't just an outpouring of love . . . it's an entire avalanche. *Lucky* feels like an understatement to describe how I feel.

Before I can slip too deep into my feelings, Austen, who has the task of keeping track of who gave which presents, holds his wide-ruled notepad in the air. "Wedding presents? Do I have to take notes on those too?"

"No, sweetie." His mother lays a reassuring

hand on his shoulder. "We'll make Graham be in charge of that tomorrow."

Graham's glare could melt steel, but it's quickly interrupted by Aunt Molly volunteering her present to be next.

"Open my tea towels!" she shouts, then claps a hand over her mouth, wide-eyed at her mistake. "Shoot. I mean, uh, open my *gift*. It could be anything at all!"

The room breaks out in laughter so loud, it drowns out Graham's permanently bad mood. When I pull two plush tea towels from Aunt Molly's gift bag, I still make sure to act surprised. Each one has a perfect letter *T* embroidered in pale pink thread. My soon-to-be new last name has never felt so official.

"Thank you, Aunt Molly," I say with a grin. "These will be so gorgeous in our kitchen."

Our kitchen, in *our* home.

Logan's apartment on the Boston Common is plenty big enough for two, so we've arranged for me to break my lease and move in with him for the duration of his contract with the Titans. After that, I'm crossing all my fingers and toes that he can secure a transfer to the Denver Avalanche, putting us just a hop, skip, and a jump from Lost Haven. It's a long shot, but crazier things have happened.

Like us falling in love in the first place.

"Speaking of kitchens, let's do my present next!"

Jillian leaps to her feet, scurrying to the pile of presents and carefully selecting the largest box from the center. She winces and grunts as she struggles to lift it, and when she places it in my lap, I can see why. The heft of it makes me recoil.

"Jeez, Mom." Logan laughs, lifting the box to take some of the weight off my thighs. "What did you get us, a box full of bricks?"

She smiles and rolls her eyes. "I guess you'll have to open it and see."

I shimmy the sheer blush bow off the box, then peel back the matte silver paper a few inches. That's all it takes for my eyes to light up with recognition. I'd know that familiar shade of aqua anywhere.

"No way," I whisper, blinking in disbelief at both the thoughtfulness and the expense of the gift. "It's just like yours."

Jillian nods, beaming at me with a huge smile, her blue eyes twinkling. "It sure is. The exact same make and model and everything."

A murmur of *what is it* makes its way through the living room until I finally peel back the paper all the way, revealing the box to everyone. It's a state-of-the-art stand mixer in aqua blue, exactly like the one Jillian used to teach me how to make bread.

Warmth fills my chest. It may be crazy, but this mixer, those memories . . . it all makes me feel like part of the family. And family is something I never thought I'd have again.

Several pairs of expectant eyes are still appraising us, so I blink away the happy tears.

"I'd never done much baking before meeting Jillian," I explain to the family, weaving my fingers into Logan's. "She taught me everything I know, which admittedly isn't very much."

"But now you can learn on your own. Open the box. I sneaked something else in there."

I turn toward Logan, letting him take over. He pops open the lid and sticks one arm inside, emerging with a spiralbound book with a laminated floral cover.

"It's a cookbook," Jillian says. "Of all the Tate family recipes."

Logan sets it in his lap, and we flip it open together. The very first recipe? Jillian's famous currant scones. Only she's renamed them *Summer's Scones*.

My throat prickles, and I swallow hard to chase the threat of tears away. I can't cry now. I'm reserving that for when I walk down the aisle tomorrow.

"Mom, this is perfect."

I can hear the rumble of emotion in my fiancé's voice, so I take his hand again, tracing the lines of his palm with my thumb.

"Absolutely perfect," I tell Jillian. "I don't know how we can ever thank you."

"Anything for my Summer-in-law," she coos. Of all the nicknames she's tried out on me, this is by far my favorite.

It takes another hour to finish opening all the presents, but no one seems to mind. We're all just so happy to be together, to swap hugs and stories and sample the different beers Graham brewed for tomorrow. The Summer Shandy will of course be the signature drink of the evening, but the complete menu of options Graham came up with could rival that of any taproom in New England.

As grumpy as he may be, I swear that man has a soft spot for me. Good thing I have every family holiday for the rest of my life to confirm that.

As for Matt and Austen, they're tipsy and playing dodgeball with wadded-up wrapping paper by the end of the brunch. That's the thing about being home. Something about it makes you act like a kid again.

"Knock it off, assholes." Graham scowls as he blocks a ball of silver wrapping paper that one of his brothers lobbed at his head. He grinds his teeth, scrunching the paper in his fist. "Keep it up, and you'll both need crutches to get down the aisle tomorrow."

"Graham!" Jillian frowns at him. "Of all days, can we not tonight?"

He opens his mouth to argue, then shakes his head and stomps toward the staircase. Logan pushes to his feet, ready to follow him, but I hold out a hand, keeping him safe at my side.

"Not today, honey," I plead. "It's not worth it."

He pauses, then heaves out a sigh, sinking back onto the couch. "You're right," he says. "You're always right."

"And don't you forget it!" Grandpa Al shouts. Suddenly, the tension is gone, replaced with more raucous laughter.

And there's that feeling again, that warmth radiating out from my chest that can only mean one thing. Even with its ups and downs, fights and all, I'm finally home at long last.

25

LOGAN

Nothing prepares you for how you'll feel on your wedding day. In fact, I don't even think feelings were mentioned in our ultra-fast wedding-planning process.

We practiced our dance moves until we wore down the carpet in the living room, and I must have rehearsed saying "I, Logan, take you, Summer" in the mirror a dozen times, paranoid that I'd somehow manage to mess up that small phrase. But there's nothing I could have done to predict the feeling in my gut as I stand here at the front of our barn-turned-brewery-turned-wedding venue, waiting for my bride to walk down that aisle.

God, if I could bottle this feeling, it would fly off the shelves.

I can only describe it as the best rush of adrenaline I've ever felt, mixed with a strange inner calm. No pre-wedding jitters or second thoughts. I've never felt more certain that this is where I belong—ready and waiting for a lifetime with Summer by my side.

I scan the wooden benches filled with familiar faces, soaking in all the love they're sending my way. We kept things small—a smattering of Tates; Summer's mentor, Les; and the minister. Just enough folks for it to feel like a special occasion without any extra faces I don't recognize.

My side is full of dark-haired, blue-eyed folks in their Sunday best, looking like they stepped out of a Kohls catalogue instead of the usual Mountain Living.

Summer's side, however, is a little sparse. Les and his wife sit quietly at the end of the second row, and I'm suddenly overwhelmed with gratitude for the man. I barely know him, but it means a lot to Summer that they came all this way. After losing her mom in that senseless accident, she has no family. We've talked about it before, but seeing it with my own eyes has my stomach in knots.

But it won't be that way for much longer. A few *I do's* from now, she'll officially be a Tate, and she'll have more family than she'll know what to do with. The thought has me grinning like a damn fool.

"Shh!"

It's almost time, but a snicker from behind me breaks my concentration. I turn to see Austen and Matt, each of them sporting a proud grin.

I follow Austen's smile toward the top of the Christmas tree behind us. Somehow, these idiots managed to swap out the star with our bride and groom wedding cake topper. It's lopsided and dumb, and somehow also fucking delightful—so very much like my family.

Out of the corner of my eye, I spot my cousin pick up Matt's guitar to quietly tune it, and my distracted thoughts settle as the soft music begins, signaling the entrance of the bride. My stomach constricts with eager anticipation.

Here comes the love of my life.

When the barn doors open, my entire body lights up like a bonfire. There she is. Summer, an absolute vision in white. With a long lace skirt floating around her and a plunging neckline that has my head swimming, *perfect* is an understatement for the woman before me. My bride. My wife. She knocks the wind out of me more than any puck ever has.

Grandpa Al is looking pretty dapper himself in a modest tweed suit and tie, albeit a little wobbly as he walks her down the aisle. It's less of a giving away of the bride in this case, and more of a welcoming home. When Summer places her long, elegant fingers in mine, I want to freeze time and hang on to this moment forever.

"Hi," she whispers soft enough so only I can hear. "I love you."

"I love you too," I whisper back.

I could say it a thousand more times, shout it for everyone to hear for hours on end. But instead, I say the only thing that's more powerful than *I love you*.

I say, "I do."

And when the minister says, "man and wife," Summer Tate becomes my family. My forever.

The reception passes by in a blur of well wishes and teary-eyed smiles. Though I somehow manage to hug everyone and thank them for coming, I can't think about anything other than Summer's hand in mine. Her wedding ring is cool against my fingers, and with every touch of her palm to mine, pride swells in my chest.

This woman is my wife. *My* wife. How I managed to pull that off, I'll never know. I've certainly changed a lot from the grumpy bastard she first met.

I can't tell you a single thing any of my brothers said in their speeches. But Summer occasionally giggles and wipes away tears with the corner of her napkin during the speeches.

"Congratulations, man," Graham grunts, smacking a hard hand against my shoulder. He nods to the bar. "Can I get you another beer?"

"No, thanks. I'm good."

Graham grumbles something about the nutty tones in the latest batch overpowering the other flavors, but I tune him out in favor of gazing across the candlelit tabletops at my wife. She's laughing with my mother, probably swapping embarrassing stories about me.

It doesn't take long for her to catch me staring. With a sly smile, she nods her head toward the door leading into the stables and gives me what I can only call bedroom eyes.

How can I resist that invitation?

"Figures," Graham mumbles, snapping me back to our conversation "You two couldn't even last an hour."

"What are you talking about?"

He levels me with a hard look. "Tell me you aren't about to sneak off together."

Shit. I guess my staring was a bit more obvious than I thought. "Uh . . ."

Before I can think of anything to say, Graham shakes his head almost mournfully and pulls a twenty-dollar bill out of his wallet. Matt appears seemingly out of nowhere, plucking his winnings from Graham's hand.

Leave it to these morons to place bets on my wedding night.

"Gross," Matt says, but the grin on his face is downright gleeful.

I roll my eyes and abandon my brothers to join Summer in the stables.

"Did anyone see you?" she asks between giggling kisses.

"Most definitely." I sigh, dragging my lips across her neck to the delicate column of her throat. God, she smells like pine and promise. "But I don't give a damn."

"Me either," she whispers, nipping at my ear and sending electricity surging through every inch of my veins.

It's almost enough for me to forget that we're in a freaking stable and about a hundred yards from all my family members. But I don't care. I could be anywhere with Summer, and I'd be the happiest man on the face of the earth.

And who knows, maybe this is our thing? We once got busy up against a chicken coop. At least the stables are vacant—we're not horse people.

But her lips on my neck distract me from those thoughts. My fingers work under her silky dress, venturing up her mile-long legs. There's a lot of dress, but I finally manage.

A few quick steps to the right, and I've got her pinned against the wooden wall, pressed against me like a second skin. Who cares if we disappear for twenty minutes? Who cares if we come back covered in hay? All I give a damn about is her skin on mine.

I've never loved formalwear more than when Summer unzips me without a single snag. She pulls me out of my pants in all of three seconds, sending a shock wave of pleasure coursing through my veins. Why the hell do I wear jeans all the time when a quickie could be *this* easy?

Even when it feels impossible for us to be any

closer, I slide my hands up her legs and scoop her up against me. She clings to me, breaking the kiss only to look longingly into my eyes as she sinks down onto my shaft, hot and liquid. My breath catches in my throat as I thrust into her, noting this moment as one I will never, ever forget.

"Logan, I . . . love you," she gasps between stifled moans.

"I love you too, Summer," I grit out, crushing my mouth to hers as we cleave to each other, riding out our releases together.

"Oh my God." Summer laughs, fighting to catch her breath.

Reluctantly, we detach from each other, and Summer puts on a stray shoe that got kicked off in all the action.

"Time for the walk of shame," she murmurs. "We're going to look insane."

I pluck a piece of straw from her hair. "We could just sneak out the back and head for our cabin, you know." I try not to sound too eager about the idea. This is her call.

"Ours?"

I nod, happy to remind her that everything that is mine is now hers. The smile I get in return is worth more than any of the wedding gifts piled high inside the house. Although I am excited to watch Summer open those later, and even more excited to pick out the home we'll fill with all our new treasures. The home we'll raise children in and grow old together. I can hardly wait.

Summer taps one pink-painted fingernail against her lower lip. "Tempting," she says with a hum. "What about your family?"

"They'll put two and two together," I say coolly. "Besides, we'll see them all at brunch tomorrow."

"And Les?"

"He's in one of the guest rooms."

She chews her lip for long enough that I almost believe she's on the fence. Finally, she relents with sparkling eyes. "Okay, rookie. Let's get outta here."

I couldn't have said it better myself.

EPILOGUE

SUMMER

"The oddest thing happened in town to-night," Logan says, shedding his coat.

I meet his eyes, and they're alight with curiosity. "What?"

"Well, we were at Duke's Tavern grabbing a beer . . ."

He joins me on the sofa in front of the fire after slipping off his boots. I nod and listen as he begins his story.

We're home for a quick spring break, visiting family in Lost Haven for three days. It's not long enough, but Logan's in the middle of the hockey season. Our visit here is so short that he felt bad about taking an evening to go out with his brothers, but I convinced him it was a good idea under the guise of brotherly bonding. Lord knows they need it—there's enough fighting between them as it is.

While the brothers were gone, Grandpa Al, Jillian, and I played cards, enjoying a lovely charcuterie board she'd put together for us to snack on. Olives and dried figs, rosemary crackers, and cheese, of course. *Lots* of cheese. I don't think I've ever eaten so much cheese.

Logan continues. "We'd just ordered our first round of beers when Ella Emerson stumbled over to our table."

"Ella?" It's a name I've never heard him mention before.

He nods. "Our neighbors, the Emersons. Three daughters. Ella's the youngest."

I didn't even realize you could consider the property on the other side of their sixty acres a neighbor, but I nod for him to continue.

"She's just turned twenty-one and probably had too much to drink, but she was with friends, so it wasn't something to worry about. Not really."

"Okay," I say slowly, wondering where this story is going.

"Except Graham was worried. Like an over-protective mother hen. First, he took off his jacket and placed it over her shoulders, even though she insisted she wasn't cold."

I raise one eyebrow, recalling a similar move from Logan, who insisted on buying me boots when I first arrived here last year and snow was starting to fly. "What was she wearing?"

"Uh, a dress, I think." He scratches at the stubble on his chin.

Actually, it's more than stubble now. He's been working on growing a beard the past few weeks at the encouragement of the guys on his team. They're making a push for the playoffs, and apparently playoff beards are a thing. I still have a lot to learn about hockey. But he's handsome both ways—clean shaven and scruffy like this.

"And then," Logan says, continuing his story, "he asked her if she had a sober ride home. She said a friend was coming by later to pick her up."

I'll admit, my interest is piqued. In all the time I've known Graham, which admittedly isn't all that long, he's never had a relationship. Not even a one-night thing, unless he's just super discreet. Which is entirely possible because Graham is one of the most guarded people I've ever met.

"He got up right then and tossed a couple of twenties on the table, and told her he was taking her home."

"Wow."

Logan touches my hair, brushing his fingers through the long strands hanging over my shoulder. I don't even think he realizes he's doing it, but he's always finding small ways to touch me. I love how affectionate he is.

"Yeah. And when Austen made a joke about Ella being too young for him, Graham looked like he was going to hit him."

I laugh. Now that sounds more like the Graham I know—settling a minor dispute with the threat of physical violence.

"He left before he even got to talk to Duke, the owner, about getting his beer on draft there. It's all he's talked about for weeks, but he didn't even wait for Duke to come by our table. It was like the second he saw Ella, his entire demeanor changed."

"How so?" I tilt my head.

"All he could focus on was getting her covered up and out of there. He threw some money on the table and then drove her home."

"He just left?"

"Yup."

"Wait, wasn't he the one who drove you all there?"

"Yup."

"So, he just stranded you?"

"Yup."

"And that's why you're late getting home?"

"Yup."

Laughing, I place my hands on Logan's scruffy face and pull him in for a kiss. His lips press lightly to mine, and a small thrill zips through me at the chaste contact. No one has ever affected me like my husband.

We talked about a long engagement, about taking our time. But in the end, we were married within a couple of months of meeting each other. When you know, you know, as they say. And I knew Logan was my forever.

We had a long discussion about our future after we got engaged. Logan plans on playing hockey for another five or six seasons. He said his plan is to retire from professional hockey by the age of thirty, and then we plan to start a family.

I'm completely on board with that plan. The idea of five years to build my practice, five years to enjoy the newlywed lifestyle I already love—it sounds perfect to me.

I'm still so thankful our paths crossed the way they did. I took a big chance coming out here to work with him, but I guess that risk paid off. I smile as he brings his arms around me and holds me close.

"I love you, Summer."

"I love you too."

We sit together for a few minutes, watching the fire while I ponder this new information about the oldest Tate brother.

I didn't think Graham was a relationship type of guy. Granted, that probably isn't going to happen with Ella, but still, it will be interesting to see how this plays out. Although him settling down would make Jillian happy. I know she worries about him.

And as fascinated as I know Logan is about this new development, he has bigger things on his mind. The season is in full swing, and his team has gotten off to a great start. In fact, all during this time away, there has been a constant stream of texts from his teammates.

It was all in good-natured fun—lots of trash talking, teasing, and banter. One particular text had him chuckling, and when I asked to see it, he warned me it was a photo of Saint mooning the camera. I opted to pass.

I guess this is their way of keeping stress levels down. Although I do wonder how exposing your bare ass to a camera accomplishes that. Still, I'm glad Logan has the guys in his life.

He rises from the couch and tugs me up with him. "Come to bed?"

We're staying in one of the cabins on the far end of the property, rather than at Jillian's house. She wanted us to stay in a guest room since it's just her and Al in the main house, but Logan politely declined. I don't think it would be prudent to risk my mother-in-law overhearing us having sex. And let's just say our bedroom activities can get a little . . . noisy. Not that I'm complaining.

But all lucid thoughts drift from my mind as Logan slowly begins undressing me.

"Need you," he whispers against my collar-bone, where he places a soft kiss. "That okay?"

We made love this morning, but I'm not about to deny him. Things are still so heated between us. I keep waiting for that to fade, but so far it hasn't.

"Yes," falls from my lips.

Once he's succeeded in leaving our clothes in a pile on the floor, he pulls me onto the bed on top of him. And a few minutes later when he joins us, I let out a gasp. Nothing has ever felt this right. A loud sigh pushes past his lips as he presses his face to my throat.

He whispers sweet words, kissing them into my skin. "You're mine, Summer."

Nothing sounds better in the world to me than that. Belonging to this man. Being part of this family.

This is all I've ever wanted in the world, and now it's mine.

Forever.

• • •

Ready for more? Up next in this series is Saint's story, and believe me, you do not want to miss this!

What to Read Next

THE REBOUND

The last thing my newly single—and pregnant—neighbor Kinley needs is a fling. So, I make it my job to protect her from guys like me.

Which is the perfect distraction, because I'm suddenly in a whole bunch of hot water.

My coach hates me. And with our team captain now watching my every move, I need to start taking things more seriously.

Forced to walk the straight and narrow or face serious consequences, I'm willing to try something new—being a good guy. But the part of this that's not an act? Helping out Kinley.

There's just one problem. The girl I'm falling for? She's the team captain's sister.

Kinley is funny and sweet and she's . . . um, *very* pregnant.

And even though my spot on this team depends on it . . . I can't let her go.

Get Two Free Books

Sign up for my newsletter and I'll automatically send you two free books.

www.kendallryanbooks.com/newsletter

Follow Kendall

Website

www.kendallryanbooks.com

Facebook

www.facebook.com/kendallryanbooks

Twitter

www.twitter.com/kendallryan1

Instagram

www.instagram.com/kendallryan1

Newsletter

www.kendallryanbooks.com/newsletter

Other Books by Kendall Ryan

Down and Dirty

Crossing the Line

Wild for You

Taking His Shot

How to Date a Younger Man

Penthouse Prince

The Boyfriend Effect

My Brother's Roommate

The Stud Next Door

The Rebel

The Rival

The Rookie

The Rebound

For a complete list of Kendall's books, visit:

www.kendallryanbooks.com/all-books/

CPSIA information can be obtained
at www.ICGtesting.com
Printed in the USA
BVHW030939170721
612164BV00007B/256